Too Hot To Handle . . .

Chiun bent down and rolled back one of Remo's pants legs and saw the redness of the skin, which contrasted to the paleness of Remo's bare arms and face and made him resemble a comic-book Indian.

"These are burns, Remo."

"Right. Burns. Whole body burned."

"Your arms are not burned. Nor is your face." Chiun examined Remo's other leg. The skin was seared. Not deeply, but thoroughly—although in some places the redness was lighter. The hairs on Remo's legs were not singed, which was strange. Remo's chest was burned also.

Chiun, who had lived more than 80 years and had confronted nothing he could not understand, felt something like a chill run along his spine.

"How were you burned, Remo?" the Master of Sinanju said urgently. "What did this to you?"

"Lights. Pretty lights. Shiny. Burns."

Then Remo's head fell forward as he collapsed. Chiun scooped him up into his arms as if Remo were a baby . . .

The Destroyer #56

Warren Murphy

ENCOUNTER GROUP

PINNACLE BOOKS   NEW YORK

For Spencer Johnson,
a friend for all the minutes

This is a work of fiction. All the characters and events portrayed in this book are fictional, and any resemblance to real people or incidents is purely coincidental.

THE DESTROYER #56: ENCOUNTER GROUP

Copyright © 1984 by Richard Sapir and Warren Murphy

An original Pinnacle Books edition, published for the first time anywhere.

First printing/June 1984

ISBN: 0-523-41566-4

Can. ISBN: 0-523-43101-5

Cover art by Hector Garrido

Printed in the United States of America

PINNACLE BOOKS, INC.
1430 Broadway
New York, New York 10018

9 8 7 6 5 4 3 2 1

ENCOUNTER GROUP

CHAPTER ONE

Amanda Bull did not believe in Unidentified Flying Objects and never gave the subject any thought whatsoever. But on the day she married John Schutz, a high school science teacher from Georgetown, she took the first step toward contact with the alien force that would transform her into an instrument of destiny. She just didn't know it.

Had someone taken her aside that day and mentioned UFOs, Amanda would have snorted, "Flying saucers? You've got to be kidding. Only morons believe that crap. Besides, I'm getting married. The only saucers I'm worried about are the ones my husband's going to wash."

And so she wed. But not before taking her father aside to give him a long-overdue piece of her mind. Even though old Edmond Bull had supported Amanda right up to her thirty-third birthday—which had been two weeks before—while she attended an endless string of women's rights conferences, ERA rallies, and protest marches, and he never complained when Amanda refused to take even a part-time job so the old man wouldn't have to work weekends to make ends meet, Amanda Bull accused her father of being selfish, insensitive, a male chauvinist pig, and an oppressor of women.

After listening openmouthed to almost an hour of strident invective, 68-year-old Edmond Bull, who had single-handedly raised Amanda after his wife had died giving birth to her, stammered, "But—but, Mandy. I've never spoken a harsh word to you in my life. Why are you saying these terrible things to me?''

''Why? You ask why?'' Amanda Bull screeched. ''I'll tell you why. In 1977 I asked you for a lousy $210.55 to fly to Kansas City for an abortion rights rally and you refused me—your own damn daughter!''

''But, dear, I told you we didn't have the money. And you know how I feel about abortion. Your poor mother—''

''Don't you dare 'poor mother' me, you hypocrite. If you hadn't selfishly gotten her pregnant, my mother would be alive today.''

''But, Mandy—''

''Forget it. I've been waiting years to tell you off to your face. Now that I have a politically conscious husband, I don't have to put up with your vicious antifeminism anymore. And after today, I don't want to see you ever again.''

And with that, Amanda Bull, armed with the courage of her convictions and knowing that she would never have to rely on her father for support again, stormed into the Church of the Overpowering Moment, and married John Schutz, the only man who ever understood her, and whom she had met at an ERA rally two years before.

All through the ceremony in the converted grocery store, old Edmond Bull wept uncontrollably, and only Amanda knew the real reason for his tears, but she told herself that her father was merely paying the price for the way he and all his male ancestors had treated women. Actually she sort of liked hearing his sobbing. Screams would have been nice too.

John Schutz and Amanda honeymooned in Los Angeles, where a hooker tried to pick up John, prompting the newlyweds to demonstrate on behalf of that city's prostitute population, ''who are being cruelly exploited by men offering large amounts of money for their services and then oppressed by the pigs simply for doing their work,'' as Amanda explained to her new husband. ''If men offered fifty dollars an hour for office work, these women wouldn't have to walk the streets.''

John Schutz agreed that it was a worthy cause—although he felt uncomfortable when two hookers in the protest line propositioned him and then stole his wallet when he declined their services. John Schutz was a feminist, too, and he understood when Amanda refused to make love on their wedding night because she was exhausted from demonstrating.

He understood when Amanda refused to wear her wedding ring because it "represented man's enslavement of womankind" but insisted that John wear his as proof of his commitment to her.

He understood when Amanda insisted that from now on, she would not use birth control because for centuries men had placed that unfair burden on women—forgetting that the prophylactic predated the Pill by several centuries.

But he had second thoughts when she announced that, in their marriage, she was to be addressed as Amanda Bull-Schutz.

"I think it would be better if you didn't, dear," John suggested quietly.

"Why not? And don't call me dear. It's degrading to my self-image."

"It's only an expression of affection, Mandy. But, really, don't you think Amanda Bull-Schutz sounds a bit . . . awkward?"

Amanda thought for a second. "Hmmmm. I see what you mean. . . ." She paced the hotel room, which gave an excellent view of 23 cubic yards of California smog. She was a tall, willowy blonde with eyes the color of a gray cat's fur, and a clear, unblemished complexion. Her only visible physical flaw was the single dark hair that grew flat along the bridge of her patrician nose, just above the tip. Although the hair annoyed her, she refused suggestions to pluck it or remove it by electrolysis because she wasn't about to do anything of the sort "just to please men and their stupid standards of female beauty." She rubbed the bridge of her nose while she thought.

"All my married friends combine their married and maiden names," Amanda said.

"Under the circumstances, I think they'll understand if you drop your maiden name," John said.

"Don't call it a maiden name. That's disgusting," she said. "It's my unmarried name. And it represents my heritage as a woman. It represents the centuries of women who have borne me."

"Your maid—unmarried name isn't your mother's name. It's your father's name," John pointed out politely.

"Are you becoming one of *them*, too?" she snapped.

He wasn't sure who *they* were, but he knew he didn't want to be one of them, so he shrugged. "I won't think less of you if you just use your unmarried name," he said.

Amanda thought quickly. What would happen if she kept her name Amanda Bull and then met someone she'd gone to college with? They might think that she had not been able to snare a husband and was still single.

"No! No! It just doesn't work. It had to be hyphenated. It has to be Amanda Bull-Schutz. There's no other way."

And so she became Amanda Bull-Schutz. It was not so difficult when they were with Amanda's feminist friends, because they seldom smiled and never laughed even among each other. But when they were with John's friends, it was more of a problem. At parties, Amanda always introduced herself in a loud voice, as if her very loudness could drown out criticism. Most people waited until she was out of earshot before snickering, but others laughed in her face—and John's face, too. This only made Amanda angrier. And the angrier she got, the more determined she was to be accepted as Amanda Bull-Schutz. She took to introducing her husband as John Bull-Schutz.

John found himself losing his friends. Before long, the

only friends he had left were Amanda's feminist friends, but after one of them tried unsuccessfully to seduce him, Amanda wouldn't allow her husband to attend any more rallies and blamed him for the incident.

Three months and sixteen days after they were joined in wedded bliss, Amanda Bull-Schutz returned home to find a note attached with a magnetic smile button to the door of the avocado-green refrigerator:

Dear Amanda,

I can't stand it anymore. The house is yours. The bank account is yours. I just want my freedom. My lawyer will contact you.

I'm sorry.

Your loving husband,
John (no Bull) Schutz

Amanda was crushed. Then her natural anger rose to the surface. She paced the floor of her model kitchen, which was equipped with year-round air-conditioning, and tore savagely at her long blonde hair.

"That creep! I gave that man everything. I catered to him. I trusted him. I shared with him. That miserable creep! There probably isn't enough money to support me for a year in that stupid bank account."

And there wasn't. Nor in Amanda's personal account either—the one her husband had set up and maintained because Amanda had demanded an account of her own so she could continue to feel independent while her husband worked.

The first thing Amanda did was to run to the Georgetown Women's Crisis Center. When the counselor there found out that Amanda hadn't been beaten or raped by her husband at any time, the counselor wanted to send her home because she was convinced Amanda was lying.

"All husbands beat their wives," explained the counselor, who had listened to horror tales of abuse of women by men for the seven years she had worked at the Georgetown Women's Crisis Center and as a result had assumed that all men were despicable and beat their wives or girlfriends regularly each Friday night.

"But John didn't," cried Amanda, who was in tears by now.

"How long have you two been married?" the counselor demanded firmly, while pretending to take notes.

"About three months."

"In that case, I'm sure your husband hadn't gotten around to beating you yet. Some men actually wait a few years before they start. It's some kind of game they play."

That fit in with Amanda's current attitude toward men, but it didn't help her situation and she said so.

"Well, I'm sorry, but there's nothing I can do for you if you haven't been raped or beaten," the counselor repeated sternly.

"But I just want someone to talk to!" Amanda cried.

"Sorry."

The next thing Amanda did was to go home to her father. She knew she couldn't afford the mortgage payments on the house her husband had left her with, so she went home telling herself that her father would take her back in a minute.

"Besides, he owes me for what he did to Mom."

Except that Edmond Bull didn't owe anyone any longer. He had died only a few weeks before.

He had written her several letters from the hospital as he lay dying, but she had torn them up unopened.

She went to their family house but found that it had been purchased by strangers a few days before. She went to the family lawyer to claim her inheritance.

"Your father had a modest number of real estate holdings and some stocks and bonds," the lawyer said.

"When do I get it?"

"You don't," the lawyer said.

"What do you mean?"

"Your father left his money in equal amounts to the American Legion, the Moral Majority, the Citizens Against Abortion, and to the local Police Athletic League," the lawyer said.

"He left me nothing, the rat bastard?"

"Well, he left you this." The lawyer handed her an envelope. Inside was a crisp new $1 bill and an itemized accounting of all the money Edmond Bull had spent on his daughter since high school, feeding her, buying her clothes, sending her to school, financing her one-woman revolution. The amount totaled $127,365.12.

"I'll fight the will," she said.

"You don't have a chance," the lawyer said.

"You're just another woman-oppressing flunky, just like my father," she said.

"Yes, indeed," the lawyer said with a smile.

Amanda was crushed. In just a few short hours, her life had been turned upside down. Amanda's faith in men—one man, anyway—had been destroyed. And her faith in women was a little shaky, too. After wandering Georgetown's student-filled streets in a confused state, she decided it had something to do with the corrupting influence of nearby Washington. Maybe some kind of conspiracy. What kind wasn't exactly clear, but lately even the women she met were as bad as the worst MCP she'd ever met. There had to be an explanation somewhere.

Because it never occurred to her that the problem might not be one of men versus women, but of human nature, Amanda decided to head west to seek a better life.

At the point when Amanda Bull, no longer Bull-Schutz, loaded her most prized possessions into a backpack and set out in search of truth and equality, she still didn't believe in flying saucers, but she unknowingly took her second step toward forces beyond her comprehension.

"Maybe if I became a lesbian . . ." Amanda mused as

she trudged backward along Interstate Highway 81 with her thumb cocked. It wasn't long before a lady trucker offered to take Amanda as far as Little Rock, Arkansas. She jumped in and began telling her tale of woe. By the time they rolled into Arkansas the next day, Amanda was wondering aloud if gay might not be the way after all. Her enthusiasm got a rude shock and turned to indignation when the lady trucker pulled over and made an aggressive pass at her.

"Keep your hands off me!" Amanda yelled. "Who do you think you are, anyway?"

"Hey, now. What was all that crap you've been feeding me since Memphis?"

"That was different! I'm not ready yet," Amanda said, and bolted from the truck. She ran off into the red oak forest, which was clotted with darkness. She was too shocked by her recent experience to fear anything that might be waiting in those woods. And so she picked her way, her flashlight chasing rabbits and owls and the shadows of rabbits and owls.

The moon, a silvery moon like a faraway dime, came up before Amanda realized she was hopelessly lost.

"Damn all men!" she said. "I think I'm only making things worse the deeper I go."

But, having no other choice, she continued on.

Her flashlight expired not long after that. Then she saw the light. It was a hazy, mellow kind of light a distance off in the trees. Low to the ground, it made the red oaks look like dark ghosts before a witch's cauldron.

Figuring the light to be a house, Amanda crept forward. But before she even got to the circle of light, a figure came out of nowhere and shone a light in her face.

"Halt!" a voice challenged. "Friend or Foes?"

"Uh . . . Friend—friend!" Amanda said. "And there's only one of me."

"Hah! Wrong answer. You should have said FOES."

"But I don't even know you," Amanda protested.

"That's okay." The light flipped up to reveal a bearded, jovial face, like a wood gnome with an acned past. "I'm Orville Sale, with FOES."

"Foes?"

"Yep. It stands for Flying Object Evaluation Center."

"Center doesn't start with an S," Amanda said.

"Well, we came up with the initials first and then had problems finding words that fit. Someone suggested Center because the C sounds like an S, so we used it but kept the initials as FOES. Anyway, that's us in the clearing yonder. We're scanning."

"Scanning what?" Amanda wanted to know.

"The skies, of course," Orville Sale said. "We do this every Thursday night."

"I don't get it," said Amanda, who didn't get it.

"Well, c'mon. I'll show you." Orville said, leading Amanda toward the clearing. "What's your name?"

"Amanda Bull-Sch—uh . . . Amanda Bull."

"Hey, all you folks! Meet Amanda."

There were about a dozen people of varying ages in the clearing. Although it was one o'clock in the morning, there were blankets and open picnic baskets on the ground, as well as a bundle of portable searchlights aimed into the sky. Most of the group had binoculars, and others were taking turns looking into the eyepiece of an eighteen-inch Newtonian telescope, which would have provided an exceptional view of the skies if it weren't for all the ground illumination. They stopped their activity long enough to wave or shout in greeting when they saw Amanda and Orville approach. Then a minor argument developed over who was next at the telescope.

"We're hoping for a Close Encounter of the First Kind tonight," Orville told Amanda with a broad, toothy smile.

"Close encounter? You mean like in that movie?"

"That's right. A Close Encounter of the First Kind is a visual sighting, a Close Encounter of the Second Kind means a landing, and a Close Encounter of the Third Kind—which is the best of them—is actual contact with alien beings from another world.

"We're talking about flying saucers, right?"

"Well," Orville said in his aw-shucks voice, "we don't call 'em that. We like to refer to them as Unidentified Flying Objects—UFOs for short." He pronounced UFOs as "U-foes." "There's been a heap of sightings in this area the last few days. That's why we're here."

"I don't believe in that crap," said Amanda, who had a distinct knack for relating to new friends.

"Look! I see one," a female voice called out suddenly.

Through the open patch of night sky directly overhead, a cluster of red and white lights could be seen moving against the stars.

"I don't hear any sound," one person whispered. "It must be a spaceship flying by magnetic power."

"I never saw anything like it before," someone in a jogging suit added, while the others scrambled to adjust the big telescope. Before they got organized enough to see that the lights belonged to a 747 flying to Nashville, the object had passed from sight.

"You people do this every Thursday?" Amanda asked.

"That's what I said," Orville grinned. "We're the Little Rock Chapter of FOES; there's dozens all over the country, though. But, zowie, wasn't that the most exciting thing you ever saw in all your life? That was the first genuine sighting in the sixteen years of our chapter—unless you count the one back in August 1975, which the Air Force claimed was the planet Jupiter."

"That's great," Amanda said. "How far to the nearest town?"

"Oh, about three miles due north. Why?"

"Because that's where I'm going. Thanks. Good-bye."

Amanda Bull never made it to town. She had barely covered three-quarters of a mile when the black Arkansas night seemed to close in on her. At first that was all she felt. A strange sensation of pressure, as if the trees were crowding close like living creatures. Then there was a heaviness in the air, but that might have been the warmth of the night.

Amanda really didn't become concerned until she heard the humming sound. Then, as it grew louder, she realized that the humming was connected with the oppressive feeling that had come over her.

She ran.

Running brought her to an open space before she could react to the sudden absence of trees. Somehow she knew that one thing she didn't wish was to be caught in a clearing. But one minute Amanda was tearing blindly through the forest and the next there was a hundred-foot clearing, and above that, suddenly, there was light.

A thousand arc lights might have generated such illumination. But she knew arc lights weren't red and green and blue and brilliant white, and they didn't cluster together like soap bubbles suspended in the air. But that was exactly what Amanda saw. A cluster of bright, globular lights floating at treetop level above her.

Amanda Bull screamed. Then the lights moved aside with a wobbling motion, and began to descend. Without a sound they descended, for the humming had stopped. There was no flame or rush of air to indicate propulsion. And through fingers held in front of her eyes, fingers that helped screen out some of the awful brilliance, Amanda saw the shape *behind* the lights—the dark shape of a squashed-down basketball.

Then the lights dimmed, and she made out the rodlike projections as they touched the ground, digging into the earth, and supporting the gently settling object.

When the object was at rest, Amanda thought she heard a voice, and the voice, she was certain, came from within the thing that had landed. The thing that looked like a flying saucer.

"Greetings," the voice called out reedily, as if the words were translated through a wind instrument, like a flute.

"Ummm . . . I don't believe in flying saucers," Amanda said in a strange voice.

"I am the World Master," the voice said, ignoring her remark.

"My—my name is Amanda Bull."

"Yes. I know," the voice said musically.

"You do?" Amanda said, her gray eyes wide with surprise.

"Yes, Amanda Bull. I have looked into your mind and seen confusion and unhappiness, but I have also seen beauty and honesty and truth."

"You have?"

"You have been chosen, Amanda Bull, to prepare the world. You shall be the instrument by which the Earth will enter into a new age."

And then Amanda Bull saw the lighted rectangle, like a window in the object's side, and the shadowy figure behind it. The figure's head didn't look quite the way a human head is supposed to. When the smooth hull beneath the figure cracked and let out golden light along three edges and a section of that hull fell forward, the voice issued from the golden interior with greater clarity.

"Enter, Amanda Bull. And discover your destiny."

And Amanda Bull walked into the beautiful light with the musical voice vibrating deep in her soul, the voice that seemed to speak the very language of her soul, and she smiled for the first time in weeks. As she disappeared into that light, she spoke two words very softly:

"I believe . . ."

CHAPTER TWO

His name was Remo and shoes annoyed him.

He was standing on the burning roof of a burning building. Tar on the rooftop was bubbling from the heat, and now the soft live leather of his shoes was starting to give off little puffs of steam, and the soles were sticking into the tar. Like strolling through quicksand, he thought.

So he kicked off the soft Italian loafers, stood in the hot tar in his bare feet and looked around through the thick haze of smoke for the man he had chased up to the roof.

He saw him on the far edge of the building. D. Desmund Dorkley was poised on the roof's edge, looking over, looking for some way to escape being roasted alive.

He obviously hadn't counted on Remo Williams. No one ever counted on Remo Williams. Who would count on a dead man?

Once he had been patrolman Remo Williams, a beat cop in Newark, New Jersey, who expected to retire on a police pension if he made it to age 55. Until he became one of the last persons to be sentenced to die in the electric chair, for the murder of a drug pusher Remo hadn't killed. He had been framed, and it wasn't until he woke up with slight electrical burn marks on his wrists and was informed that the chair had been rigged not to kill him, that Remo Williams learned who had set him up.

It had been the United States government—or, rather, a secret organization within that government known only as CURE. Remo had been chosen as America's secret enforcement arm to handle an out-of-control crime situation before that situation swamped American democracy.

"Then I'm not dead?" Remo had asked.

"Yes, you are," he was told. "For all intents and purposes."

And he was. Remo Williams, an orphan, had officially ceased to exist. He became just Remo, whom CURE had code-named "the Destroyer," and so began intensive training designed to make the ex-cop a human weapon. Remo had had no choice, but he went through with the whole deal, and it had changed him in ways even Remo didn't always understand. But all that was long ago, and all D. Desmund Dorkley knew was that a skinny guy with very thick wrists was running barefoot toward him, and there was no expression of pain in the man's eyes as there should have been. The eyes just looked dead.

For D. Desmund, it was to have been an ordinary torch job. A pile of rags in a corner of an old warehouse, a can of gasoline and a flick of a Bic. No problem.

Until the unexpected Remo Williams stepped out of the shadows and asked, "Got a light, pal?"

That was just as the rag pile went orange with a *whooosh!* D. Desmond, who never carried a gun because loud noises frightened him, dived out the nearest exit, which unfortunately led to the roof. It was a fundamental mistake. You do not go up into a building that is about to go up. You get out. But something about the cold, dead eyes of Remo Williams unnerved D. Desmund. So, he made his first professional mistake.

It was to have been an ordinary job for Remo Williams, too. He hadn't counted on the arsonist getting the fire started, but Remo was delayed because his trainer had insisted on accompanying him on an ordinary hit.

"Damn Chiun," Remo muttered as he shifted to a less

hot part of the warehouse roof, where the tar wouldn't stick to his feet. There, the roof was only hot enough to broil a steak, not cook the skin from his feet in sliding chunks. Remo wore a black T-shirt that left his arms bare. It was the lesser evaporation of sweat from his left arm that told Remo that it was cooler to his left, and so he veered left.

Remo could do these things because of his training. It worked this way: Remo ran in a long-legged stride in which only one foot touched the ground at a time. The principle depended entirely on rhythm, which is what made Remo's movements look so graceful, as if his feet floated from motion to motion. The rhythm demanded that Remo keep moving and that one foot remain in the air for the exact length of time the other touched the hot roof surface. With each step, Remo felt the brief flash of heat signaling contact, but only long enough to touch, find traction, and propel him forward another step. Then the other foot took over. Yes, Remo felt the heat but, no, Remo's feet were not burned. They were not in contact with a heat source long enough to be burned. As for the pain, what little Remo felt in the soles of his bare feet was drawn up his legs, through the nerves, where it was diffused into a tingling sensation. Correct breathing technique enabled Remo to handle pain in this manner.

It was not much different from the way Hindu fire walkers moved over hot coals—except that they had the technique secondhand and were sometimes burned. Remo had the technique from its originators, which is to say he had it in its pure form and not the Hindu style, which depended in part on the heat-absorbing properties of human sweat and sometimes on artificial salves. And he knew that as long as only one foot touched at a time and he didn't break stride, he could run across the burning roof safely.

Remo knew how to make the technique work, but he didn't understand *how* it worked. His trainer understood, but Remo had a long way to go before he completely mastered the art of Sinanju, of which fire walking was but a part. On the other hand, he had only a short way to go across the roof, and he got to the cooler edge just as D. Desmund Dorkley, with a horrified scream, tried to jump out and down to the next roof.

"Uuurk," said D. Desmund, when he found himself hanging in midair by his green jacket collar, his yellow bow tie looking like a bright, vampiritic butterfly at his throat.

"Let me go. Let me go. God, put me down," D. Desmund screeched. His legs kicked like a swimmer's over empty space, and his blond hair was limp with sweat. He didn't look like a man who had torched a museum, a church, two office buildings, a fast food restaurant and a school for the blind in just three weeks, and all in the Baltimore area, which showed up on CURE's computers as an aberration significant enough to call for drastic attention. Those same computers had worked out a probability pattern that pinpointed the warehouse as the arsonist's next target so that Remo Williams could be there.

And now Remo, who had simply extended his hand and caught D. Desmund's coat collar, stood on the edge of the roof and held the arsonist out at arm's length. Although Remo did this casually, it didn't seem possible. For one thing, Remo's arm was too thin and held at too awkward an angle for him to be able to stand on a precipice and hold up a struggling man without both of them toppling over the edge.

If D. Desmund hadn't been scared completely out of his mind, he would have realized that fact and possibly pointed this out to Remo Williams.

Remo, had he been so inclined, might have informed him that his arm really wasn't holding up a 200-pound man by main strength. No, it just looked that way to Western eyes because Westerners always thought in terms of just using their arms and then only the muscles in those arms, as if muscles alone provided strength and weren't really simply a system of pulleys—which was exactly what a muscle was when you thought about it. A pulley.

No, Remo was holding D. Desmund up with Remo's entire body—from the strong toes, which hooked over the roof edge for purchase, to the straight legs and locked knees; and to the stiff spinal column, which provided a fulcrum for the arm, which was held in position by muscle tension, but whose strength really came by the bones within that arm. Balance had something to do with it all. Balance was important in Sinanju, but strength came from the correct alignment of bones that interlocked and spread the dragging weight of D. Desmund's body throughout Remo's body. Balance, bones, muscles, and breathing. All of Remo functioning in perfect harmony with its parts and creating a unity which was greater than the sum of those parts, tapping Remo's inner potential. This was Sinanju.

And so D. Desmund did not fall to his death, taking Remo with him.

When D. Desmund finally stopped screaming and flailing, and said, "Oh dear God almighty" once weakly and shut his eyes, Remo hauled him back to the roof edge, careful not to disturb the harmony of his own body.

"I want the truth," Remo said, after his captive again opened his eyes.

"Sure," D. Desmund said. "You got it. Any truth you want. Just name it."

"Good. I'm glad you're being cooperative. Why did you set that fire?"

"I didn't set any fire," D. Desmund told him.

"I saw you, remember?"

"Oh. That's right."

"Now, why did you do it?"

"I didn't," D. Desmund said with a straight face.

"Right," said Remo. "Let's try a different approach, okay?"

"Okay," said D. Desmund eagerly.

"Listen carefully," Remo said. "You're going to have one chance to answer this question, and then I'm going to push you off this roof. Okay?"

"Okay," repeated D. Desmund, who was as frightened as he'd ever been in his life, which meant he was very, very frightened.

"Good. Stay with me, now. Here's the big question: Did you torch all of those buildings because someone paid you or because you wanted to?"

"Because I wanted to. I like to watch stuff burn."

"That's fine. Thank you for leveling with me. Goodbye." And Remo pushed D. Desmund off the roof.

But D. Desmund, acting by reflex, grabbed Remo's thick right wrist, which felt like a skin-covered girder.

"Wait a minute—you said if I answered your question you wouldn't push me."

"No, no," Remo corrected. "You weren't listening. I didn't say 'You're going to have one chance to answer this question *or* I'm going to push you off this roof.' I said, 'You're going to have one chance to answer this question and *then* I'm going to push you off this roof.' "

"But that's not Fa—AAAAIIIRRRR . . ." said D. Desmund just before he went splat on the hard pavement below.

"That's the biz, sweetheart," said Remo as he jumped across to the next roof and slid down its brick surface like a spider to join the kimono-clad individual who was waiting for him.

"Hear, hear," said Chiun, who was Remo's trainer and, although 80 years old, the most dangerous man on earth. "Excellently done, Remo." He was a small, frail Korean with clear hazel eyes in a wrinkled old face to which clung tiny wisps of hair above each ear and from his chin. A black night kimono concealed most of his form.

Remo, who was not used to praise from his teacher, nevertheless accepted the words graciously. "You do me great honor, Little Father."

"Yes," said Chiun. "Your technique, especially on the burning roof, was exemplary. Your feet are not even singed."

"I lost my shoes," replied Remo, who was becoming suspicious.

"Shoes are shoes, but correct technique is art. It is beauty. It is perfection. And you only recently were given the gift of fire walking."

"Yeah, but the firebug managed to torch this place before I got to him," Remo pointed out.

Chiun shrugged. "It is unimportant in the face of your skill. Besides, this structure is ugly. Someone should burn them all."

"Yeah, right," said Remo vaguely. "Can we continue this back at the hotel? The fire department will be here any minute now."

"Very well, then," said Chiun, a smile multiplying the wrinkles of his old face. "Let us return home."

"We will have duck tonight," Chiun said when they had entered the suite of their Baltimore hotel, which was one of the best in the city even though it was only two blocks away from a peep show parlor. For some reason, although the city of Baltimore had a waterfront area in which its adult entertainment establishments were congregated, there were few sections of the city not blighted by massage parlors and adult bookstores.

"I think duck in apricot sauce would be appropriate," Chiun added, humming happily to himself as he disappeared into the kitchenette.

"I've gotta tell Smith the firebug was working on his own," Remo said, picking up the phone. Smith was Dr. Harold W. Smith, the director of CURE and Remo's employer, although Smith was ostensibly the director of Folcroft Sanitarium in Rye, New York, from which he and his batteries of computers secretly ran CURE. Because Smith was waiting in Rye for Remo's report, Remo called a number in North Quincy, Massachusetts, which instantly rerouted his call through Blue Ball, Pennsylvania, but which rang a secure phone on Smith's desk.

"Remo," Smith's lemony voice demanded before Remo could so much as say hi. "What happened? I have a report the target warehouse was torched."

"Do you have a report that a body was found next to the warehouse?" Remo asked, wondering how Smith's voice could sound as bitter as a lemon wedge and as dry as a graham cracker both at the same time.

"No," Smith said.

"Well, there was. And besides, the building was ugly. So get off my case," said Remo before he hung up.

When Chiun returned a few minutes later, he was still humming, so Remo decided to get to the bottom of that, too.

"Is there some reason for this celebration I should know about?" he asked suspiciously.

Before he answered, Chiun stepped over to his sleeping mat, which had been set in the middle of the floor, and settled onto it like a leaf falling from an autumn tree.

"Yes, my son," Chiun said, his long fingernails tapping together happily. "Come, sit at my feet. We must talk. This is a happy day."

"Why?" asked Remo, even as he sat on the floor.

"Because, my son, you have come far in Sinanju. Because you are about to take a major step forward in Sinanju, and I am pleased with you."

Remo thought a moment. "I thought I'd taken a major step about a year ago. Remember? The Dream of Death? You told me then I'd be in this phase for a long time."

"This is true, Remo," Chiun said, his voice solemn. "You are still young in the eyes of Sinanju and must walk the traditional path. But today you showed me that you are ready to move forward along that path more swiftly.

To run ahead, but without straying from that path. Your work with the fire walking told me this.''

"It is a good technique," Remo said. He was debating whether or not to add "taught by an excellent teacher" when Chiun said, "Yes, a good technique, and taught by an excellent teacher. But you know this. What you do not know, for I have not told you, is that fire walking is not usually taught to one as young as you. But in ten years you have absorbed better than any Korean what I have taught you of Sinanju. This gives me hope that certain other lessons can be taught ahead of their proper time. This is important, Remo, because the more you know, the safer is your life and mine, and it is upon our safety and skills that my poor village depends. You are their future, after me. And one day you will be the Master of Sinanju instead of me. Thus, you are ready for a new technique.''

Remo had listened many times to the story of the poor village of Sinanju on the West Korean Bay, which lent out its best men as hired assassins to the great thrones of history so that starvation would not force the village to "send its babies home to the sea" because there was not food for them. The House of Sinanju developed the assassin's art of Sinanju—which was the source of all lesser martial arts—into a tradition that Remo and Chiun currently carried on in service to CURE. Remo just nodded and asked flatly, "Which technique, Little Father?"

Instead of answering, Chiun made as if to stand up and, legs poised under his kimono, sent his stiffened index finger flashing out and snipped off a lock of Remo's dark hair before Remo could react.

Before the lock fell to Remo's thigh, Chiun had seated himself again, arms folded.

Remo, his reflexes blindingly fast for a human being, caught himself in mid-strike. He had been too slow blocking Chiun's thrust, and the tips of his manicured fingers froze a centimeter in front of Chiun's parchment countenance.

"I am still reigning Master," said Chiun, amused that Remo's counterthrust had been initiated before Remo became conscious of the need to defend or strike. It was only Remo's brain catching up with his reflexes that stopped the death blow.

The lock of hair fell to Remo's crossed thigh as he dropped his arm.

"You know the art of the Killing Nail," said Chiun.

"Yeah. It's not restricted to Sinanju. Others have used it, too."

"And animals," added Chiun. "The fingernail is a natural tool. Before the club, there was the nail. But Sinanju, realizing the power of the nail properly used, cultivated the growing of the nail to a certain length, learned how to harden it through diet and exercise, and used the nail as it was meant to be used. To perform our art."

While he spoke, Chiun separated his hands and displayed them, palms inward, so that Remo could see the long, slightly curving knives that grew from Chiun's fingers and that Remo knew could open a man's jugular. Remo knew this because he had seen Chiun do that.

"Older Masters have traditionally taken to the use of the Killing Nail. It is the symbol of the ultimate assassin, the man whose weapons grow from his body and, if broken, will grow back. The Knives of Eternity, they are called."

"Little Father . . ." Remo began.

Chiun raised one delicate nail for silence. "Although you are young and a white, Remo, you are ready to take up the weapons of the eldest Masters. You are ready to let your nails grow. It is a happy day."

"Little Father, I cannot," Remo said quietly.

"Cannot? Cannot?" Chiun squeaked questioningly. "Do not be fearful of this honor, Remo. You need only trust me. I will guide you through the most difficult stages."

"Little Father, I am not ready for this."

"But you are ready, Remo. I know this," Chiun said firmly.

When Remo just sat there uncomfortably, Chiun was puzzled. "What troubles you, my son?"

"It is not my way to wear my fingernails long," Remo said quietly.

"Way?" snapped Chiun. "Way? Sinanju is your way. You are a Master of Sinanju. And the Killing Nail is the way of Sinanju. I do not understand you."

"In America," Remo explained, knowing that Chiun would not understand American customs, or else would dismiss them as unimportant if he did, "men clip their nails short. They do not wear their nails long. Only women do. It is considered unmanly to have long fingernails."

"I know this. Have I not lived in your uncivilized country since before our first meeting?"

"Then you understand what I am trying to tell you, Little Father," Remo said hopefully.

"No. I understand only that I am talking to an idiot. Remo, I am offering you something no one of Sinanju has ever been offered so young. Something no white could ever comprehend, and what obviously no white will ever appreciate. Especially you, who could not even stop a fat white fire-insect from destroying an important and beautiful building." At that point, Chiun lapsed into abusive Korean in which the phrase "pale piece of pig's ear" was the least offensive remark made.

Remo knew there would be no talking to Chiun now, and there wasn't.

"I apologize, Little Father. Perhaps when I am older. Perhaps if we survive and that day comes when I take over as reigning Master—maybe then I will be able to do this thing."

"Why not now?" Chiun demanded in English.

"Because the work that I do for Smith calls for secrecy. That is why I am dead."

"You are dead because you are the dead night tiger," Chiun snapped back, forgetting that by acknowledging Remo as the dead night tiger of Sinanju—the white man legend had foretold would be trained as the greatest Master of them all and the avatar of Shiva, the Destroyer—Chiun was acknowledging Remo's worthiness in the eyes of his ancestors.

"Maybe. But I was made to appear dead because I have been given the sword of my country to carry into battle, and it is a sword that must be carried in secret."

"A paper sword," Chiun scoffed.

"The Constitution, yes. My job is to operate outside the Constitution so that it will survive and my country will not fall."

"And so you dishonor your sword each time you wield it." Chiun spat on the floor. "How white. How American."

"Nevertheless, it is my sword. And if the hand that carries that sword becomes conspicuous, then the man will become known and his sword will be taken from him, along with his life. Where will that leave America? Or Sinanju?"

"I would train another. One with fingernails."

"But you have trained me. And you have made a contract with America so that I can carry out America's work—in secret."

"Do not remind me of my shame. Do not remind me that I have been forced to train a white meat-eater in the greatest of all professions, that of assassin, and that the greatest house of assassins has been reduced to this. I have trained you, Remo, because that is my obligation, because you learned well—up to a point—and because I had mistakenly thought you possessed the soul of a Korean. But I now know this is untrue. The Korean soul is hard like bamboo, and the fingernail grows from that hard soul. You obviously have a white soul, soft and like mist. When you die, your body will decay, and the wind will dissipate your pale, wispy soul, as happens to all whites when they die. But Korean souls are hardy. They live on. Yours will not.''

"Bulldooky," said Remo, who wasn't sure how much of this to believe, nor how much of it Chiun himself believed.

CHAPTER THREE

Crouching in the grass before the barbed-wire-topped
fence, Amanda Bull felt a surge of exhilaration flow
through her willowlike body. The feeling, which had been
coming on since dusk, had grown more intense as she drove
the official FOES van containing members of the Little
Rock, Arkansas, chapter of the group, dressed in Army
surplus fatigues with firearms purchased at Sears, Roe-
buck, and their grim faces blackened with the rubbings
from burned Gallo wine corks. It was both a swelling of her
heart and a burning in the pit of her stomach, this feeling
Amanda felt. Sometimes she thought the feeling was fear;
other times it felt like the purest kind of excitement
imaginable, like what Amanda imagined an orgasm felt
like. Amanda had never had an orgasm, although she
thought she'd come close once, while listening to Betty
Friedan speak at a convention.

But now, flat on the grass, a .22 Swift rifle cradled in
her arms and the clear Arkansas moonlight reflecting off
the RESTRICTED AREA sign on the fence before her too-
bright eyes, Amanda Bull realized exactly what the feeling
was.

It was power, pure unadulterated power. And she loved
it.

Power had come to Amanda Bull only a week before, in
the forests of Arkansas amid the smell of apple blossoms,
when the strange voice from the UFO had beckoned her,
irresistibly, to enter. There had been no time to run away,

or even to think. There was just that reedy voice, which had seemed to speak to her very soul, as if the owner of that voice knew her innermost thoughts and voiced them, but in a new way. A way that was not confused or fearful, but strong and intelligent and wise.

So Amanda had entered the spaceship. She found it full of golden light and shiny metallic surfaces, and when Amanda had oriented herself, she realized she stood in an outer chamber of the ship, but that its other occupant remained within the inner chamber. She could see a pebbled-glass rectangle, like a window in a drive-in bank, which had light coming from the other side—the inner chamber of the ship. Amanda peered in, but the pebbled glass defeated her vision.

Then a shadowy figure stepped up to the glass from the other side.

"Oh. There you are," Amanda had said. She tried to make out details of the creature, but the thick glass broke and distorted the outline, which was backlit so that even its color was impossible to figure out. But Amanda thought she saw feelers or antennae protrude from the bulbous head, and she shivered.

The voice spoke again.

"I have come across a great distance, Amanda Bull. I am an emissary from a distant world, one that circles the star known to your people as Betelgeuse."

"Beetle juice?" Amanda said wonderingly.

"Yes. That is how it is pronounced."

"Who are you?"

"I told you. I am the World Master. I have been dispatched to this planet to teach. I am a teacher. And you are my first pupil, whom I have chosen for a historic task."

"Task?"

"Through you, a new age will dawn on this troubled planet. An age without fear, without weapons, without hate. For I have been sent to purge this planet of a great evil. Once this evil has been eradicated, peace will return to this tiny world. Gone will be war, gone crime, gone poverty; gone will be—''

"Sexism?" Amanda said hopefully.

"Yes, sexism. That terrible injustice has long ago been banished from my world. My world is a paradise, as are other worlds I have touched, as will be the Earth when our work is completed, yours and mine, Amanda Bull. But I must have your help.''

"Why me?" asked Amanda, who was still getting used to believing in flying saucers.

"Because, Amanda Bull, you have been watched and are known to me as a worthy instrument. You can breathe the atmosphere of this world. You can walk its streets freely. I cannot. I must remain in the control core of my ship, where I can breathe the air of my world until the moment of destiny has arrived. Until then, I must remain hidden. My existence must be known to only a few, for there are those who, not understanding, may attempt to capture or kill me before my teachings have borne fruit.''

"I understand," Amanda said, wondering if the alien had noticed the ugly hair on the bridge of her nose.

"You know there are grave things wrong with the world you live in. These things can be changed. By you. With my help. Are you ready, Amanda Bull?''

"I—I think I am. Yes . . . I know I am. What's first? What do we change first? We can dump those bastards in Washington and replace them with friends of mine. Or—''

"None of those things," the World Master said. "There is only one task to be undertaken. All the rest will follow naturally.''

"Yes?" Amanda said expectantly.

"You must," the reedy voice told her, "destroy all of the nuclear weapons on this planet.''

"Uh. Ugh. *All* of them?''

"Starting with America's missile systems.''

Amanda suddenly felt very sick. Taking on the U.S. military establishment wasn't exactly an appealing thought.

"There are a lot of missiles," she said weakly. "Hundreds, maybe."

"Thousands. That is why you must organize preparation groups for the task. You will be Preparation Group Leader Amanda Bull. You will recruit the groups. You will direct them. I will supply the tools and advise you."

"Where am I going to get followers?"

"Not far from here are several who will follow you. You have met them. I watched you. And when we descend from the skies, you and I, to fulfill their greatest desire, to make contact with beings from another world, they will follow. Are you agreeable?"

"Yes . . . definitely," said Amanda, who liked the idea of being in charge of something—especially of something as big as this. "Just one question: are you a man or a woman?"

"On my world, those words are meaningless. I am a person."

And for the second time that night, Amanda Bull smiled. "I'm glad," she had said. "Now I know everything's going to be all right."

It hadn't been hard to convince the Little Rock, Arkansas chapter of FOES. Not when a spacecraft floated down upon them, as if it were weightless. The World Master had told Amanda that the lightness of the ship was produced by antigravity generators. Solar powered, of course. At first the sky watchers, confronted with the very thing they searched for, scattered in a blind panic. But Amanda called out to them. As the ship alighted, its lights dimming enough for her to be seen, Amanda stepped into view.

"Hey! It's that blonde," someone shouted. "The one with the hair on her nose."

And one by one the others drifted back, while Amanda

explained about the World Master from Betelgeuse and the mission she had been given, the mission they were invited to share. Suddenly they weren't frightened anymore. They were eager.

"We want to see him," they shouted like kids at recess. "Let's see the alien."

"Here's not an alien," someone else cut in. "He's what you call an *extra*-terrestrial."

"No, he's an ancient astronaut."

But when a rectangle of pebbled glass showed suddenly in front of the object on the ground, and the torso of the creature within showed itself weirdly, a hush gripped the group as if they had been asphyxiated. The World Master spoke no words, but everyone saw it wave two hands, and everyone saw that those hands were both on the right side of its body.

"Oh, wow," said Orville Sale. "A real extraterrestrial. A genuine creature from Out There. Hey, everybody! We're all contactees now," meaning that they could claim contact with alien beings.

"Yeah, but I'm not so sure about this missile stuff," said Lester Gex, who ran a secondhand bookstore in Damascus, Arkansas, and who, although a member in good standing with FOES, sometimes thought the group had more than its share of wackos. "What I mean is, this could be serious business. What if we here start disarming America and over there in Russia, they get wind of this and decide this is their chance to blow us all away?"

"The World Master has already explained that to me," Amanda called out quickly. We're going to operate in secret. Like a commando team. The government will be too embarrassed by our success to dare let any of this get into the papers. That way, the Russians won't know a thing until we begin to work on their weapons."

"I still don't like it," said Lester Gex. "I'm leavin'."

Lester Gex walked ten paces in his Wrangler boots when a silver tube popped out below the port in the spaceship, and a cold blue pencil of light licked out and dropped him in his tracks, a burnhole just over the eighth dorsal vertebra of his back. He never made a sound. He was dead.

"No one must be allowed to interfere with the dawn of the new era of peace and goodness that will be Earth's once we have prepared the human race," the World Master said musically.

"That's right," Amanda Bull said sternly.

"Oooh," a woman said, looking at the body, from which a curl of stinking smoke rose. "It was just like a laser."

"Except it was blue," Orville Sale pointed out. "Lasers are red, so it couldn't have been a laser, even though it burned Les like one."

"Yes, that's right."

After that, there were no more problems.

That had been a week ago. A week in which to arm and train Preparation Group One and take them out to scout their intended targets. The World Master gave the orders, which were relayed by Amanda Bull. Once each night, she drove out alone to a prearranged spot where the ship was always waiting, to report and receive new orders. The World Master always received her from behind the pebbled glass. Last night Amanda had reported that Preparation Group One was ready. Or, as she put it, "as ready as they're ever going to be."

"Very good, Preparation Group Leader Amanda Bull. Your first target will be the 55th Missile Wing of the United States Air Force. Here are your instructions."

Amanda subsequently learned that a missile "wing" was a loosely grouped cluster of missiles buried in scattered silos. The 55th Wing was deployed in a fan between 30 and 60 miles north of Little Rock. Because the silos, each holding a 103-foot Titan II missile, were deployed over such a wide area, they would have to attack them one at a time, retreat, and move on to the next target. It was not going to be easy, but as Amanda led Preparation Group One to within a few yards of the first missile site without being challenged by anyone, she thought that maybe it would not be all that hard, either.

"Everybody keep down," Amanda hissed to the others.

From the highway, the site seemed to be nothing more than an acre of land, fenced off, in which carefully trimmed grass grew. There were no buildings visible, just the sliding concrete silo roof set low to the ground and, not far from it, another concrete structure that was too squat to be a building. This contained electronic detection devices that were hooked up to the radar scoops set at intervals behind the perimeter fence.

"Those thingies must be radar," whispered Lucy Lamar, a 32-year-old housewife who weighed 169 pounds and looked as if her scalp was growing stubby horns under her knit cap. This was because she hadn't had time to take the curlers out of her hair earlier that evening. Until a week ago, she had fervently believed that flying saucers were the advance force of an invasion fleet that lurked just beyond the moon, waiting for the proper moment to strike—which she knew would be on April 28, 1988, because she had read that in an article in *UFO Pictorial Quarterly*.

"Yeah," said Amanda. "We don't have to worry about those. They're there to detect incoming missiles."

"Then why aren't they pointed into the sky?" asked Orville Sale. "Look at them. They're all pointing out, not up."

"Maybe they're resting," someone offered hopefully.

"Never mind about the stupid radar," Amanda snapped. "Orville! Get to work on that fence, with the wire cutters. The rest of you cover him."

Orville sneaked forward and attacked the chain links of the fence with the wire cutters while the remainder of the group hunkered together nervously, bunching up in exactly the manner soldiers in Vietnam were taught never to do because one machine gun could take them all out with a single burst.

Orville got seven entire links open and was working on the eighth when a voice called out of the darkness, "You there! This is a government installation. Stand where you are and don't move!"

"A guard!" Amanda said. "Cut him down, somebody."

When no one made a move, Amanda brought her .22 Swift up, sighted and fired. The guard went down, moaning. Probably no one was more surprised than Amanda herself, who had never hit a target in the week since she'd purchased the weapon.

"Okay," she yelled. "We've lost the element of surprise, so we've got to move fast."

They got through the fence just as a siren whined somewhere, and hidden lights came on like sprays of white blood.

They got as far as the octagonal silo roof sitting on its sliding track before the other guards, who emerged from the underground control center, opened fire. This time no one gave any warning. The brittle snapping of automatic weapons sounded like faraway firecrackers, only they weren't faraway, and the bodies began to make small piles next to the missile silo.

"Don't just stand there, you morons!" Amanda screeched. "We're under attack. Fire back!" To demonstrate, she fired straight up into the air where the bullet, meeting nothing but air resistance, lost momentum and fell from such a height that when it struck Orville Sale on the top of his head, he collapsed, seriously wounded.

The others got organized and started shooting at shadows or into the night.

Meanwhile, Amanda began applying the puttylike plastique explosive charge to the lip of the silo cover. The World Master had given her the stuff, along with instructions on its use, saying that it was a specimen once stud-

ied on his home planet—which certainly explained where
he got it, Amanda thought as she set the timer.

"Run, run! It's going to blow!" Amanda yelled, following her own instructions.

Everyone scattered who could, some into the fire from
the guards. After counting to 10, Amanda yelled,
"Dive!" and at the count of 20 the silo went *crump!*

Amanda ran back and was disappointed to see that only
one corner of the silo roof had cracked loose. And a small
corner at that. A sharp-edged crack showed, but it was
too small. "Damn, damn, damn. Not enough explosive."
Then she saw the smooth mouth going down into the silo,
which she hadn't seen before. Her flashlight didn't show
any sign of the Titan II missile, but that didn't bother
Amanda. A hole was a hole, after all.

Out of her backpack she extracted a three-pound wrench
with which she was going to disable the missile. She had
chosen a three-pound wrench because she had read about
an accident in which a technician had dropped a three-
pound wrench socket down a silo, which ruptured the
first-stage fuel tank and blew a Titan missile completely
out of its silo. Amanda couldn't find a three-pound wrench
socket—whatever that was—but she figured an ordinary
wrench would do just as well.

She dropped the wrench in, heard it bang off the side of
something metallic, and ran for all she was worth.

"The missile's going to explode, everybody! The missile's going to explode!" she cried. "Preparation Group
One, follow your leader!"

But when she got outside the fence, Amanda realized
that Preparation Group One would never follow anyone
again. They were all dead or wounded or flat on the ground
under the guns of frantic Air Force guards.

With bitter tears in her eyes, Amanda drove off in the
waiting van. "At least we got the missile," she told herself, and watched the rearview mirror for the flash she
knew would come.

But when the flash didn't come and there was no distant boom or thump, Amanda knew that she had failed utterly.

"Next time," she vowed, "I'll know to use fewer men. They always ruin everything."

CHAPTER FOUR

The last person in the world Remo Williams wanted to see for breakfast was Dr. Harold W. Smith. Chiun had been giving Remo the silent treatment since the night before, a silence broken often by mutterings in Korean, all of which had to do with Remo's worthlessness and all of which Remo had heard many times before.

Remo decided that this time he'd just ignore Chiun until the old Oriental got over his snit. So Remo had gone to sleep early and then rose early to do his exercises. When Chiun woke up, he changed from his sleeping robe to his golden day kimono when Remo wasn't looking, and then left the hotel without a word.

After Chiun left, there was a single knock at the door, and Dr. Smith entered without waiting for Remo to answer.

"Remo," Smith said in his emotionless way. It was supposed to be a greeting, but it came out sounding as though Smith had read an item off his shopping list. Usually Remo and Smith communicated over scrambled phone lines or through mail drops. The security of CURE depended on their keeping apart. But it had been some time since CURE's security had been breached, and when it had happened, the breaches had been the result of weak links in CURE personnel who didn't even know they worked for CURE or by mechanical malfunctions in

Folcroft computers. These problems had been corrected, and because Smith was only the anonymous director of a New York State research institution, he had grown more confident about personal contact when necessary.

"Don't bother knocking, Smitty" Remo said as Smith brushed by, wearing the inevitable uniform of gray suit, white shirt, Dartmouth tie, and leather briefcase. He was a plain-looking man in his sixties, boringly balding, and the type of human being who considered sweating a serious lapse in self-discipline—in himself and others. Remo had never seen Smith sweat. He couldn't remember ever seeing him not wearing his gray suit, either.

"Chiun left the door open," Smith said, opening the briefcase on the breakfast nook table.

"Yeah, he's unhappy with me again."

"You should really treat him with more respect. He's your trainer and very valuable to us."

"He's more than my trainer. He's the only family I ever had, and he'll walk all over me if I let him, so can the advice. I'll handle him any way I want." Remo was more upset with Smith than he had been in a long time. The idea of a dry, emotionless bastard like Smith lecturing Remo on his personal relationship with Chiun had struck a nerve.

"He passed me in the lobby and said you had refused the next stage of your training. This is a serious matter. We pay Chiun's village an enormous sum of money each year to retain his services."

"First of all, it's not all that much money. A lot, yeah, but he could do better doing tricks on TV than working for you."

"Chiun would not do that. He belongs to an ancient line of assassins. He would do no other work, no matter what the payment. So why don't you take the next stage of your training?"

"Okay," Remo said cheerily. "You know what Chiun wants me to do now? He wants me to grow my fingernails as long as his. It's a stage of Sinanju reserved for Masters his own age, but he thinks I'm ready to try it now. I always wanted long nails. You'll love it, Smitty. I'll go around scratching our enemies' eyes out. Me and my fingernails. Chiun and his kimonos and steamer trunks. Maybe we'll all join the circus.''

"I see your point," Smith said with a nervous cough. "I'll speak to Chiun. But right now we have a potentially serious situation on our hands.''

"Don't we always?" said Remo. "What now?" He still wanted to argue about Chiun, and now they were talking about something new. Only Smith could be both agreeable and aggravating at the same time.

"Last night there was a raid on one of our nuclear missile sites," Smith said. "A group of about a dozen people, lightly armed, attacked the site and attempted to destroy a Titan missile. They damaged the silo roof and dropped a three-pound wrench into a flame-defector vent, which carried it harmlessly past the missile, fortunately.''

"A three-pound wrench?" Remo said. "Why not a five-pound bag of potatoes?''

"You might remember. There was an accident several months ago. A Titan missile was blown out of its silo when a maintenance technician dropped a three-pound wrench socket, and it ruptured a fuel tank. The explosion tossed the warhead about 200 yards away. These people, for want of a more imaginative idea, were trying to imitate that accident.''

"Just who are these clowns?''

"That's the worrisome part. They appear to be ordinary citizens with no criminal records or obvious motives for wanting to disable an American nuclear missile. Only two of them survived. They claim to have been acting upon orders of an individual whose name they don't know, who has some plan to bring peace to the world through forced disarmament. They call him the World Master. By Master, they seem to mean teacher.''

"World Master?"

"Our computers have nothing on any person using that name," Smith said, and Remo thought he heard a trace of bitterness. Smith's computers were CURE's first line of offense, defense, and intelligence gathering. It upset him when they failed.

"I don't get it," Remo said. "Some kind of nuclear disarmament group gone bonkers?"

"No, these people have no such affiliations in their backgrounds. In fact, their only link is a strange one. They belong to an organization known as FOES."

"Terrorist?"

"No. It stands for Flying Object Evaluation Center . . . hmmm, that can't be right," Smith murmured, looking at the file again. "At any rate, their only known purpose is to gather and record sightings of Unidentified Flying Objects."

"Are we talking about flying saucers?" Remo asked.

"Precisely. A group of UFO buffs have taken it upon themselves to disarm America, missile by missile."

"You caught them all. So what's the problem?"

"As far as we *know*, we caught them all. But we found no trace of the van they used to reach the missile site. And there are other chapters of FOES in other states. If this is a national movement within that organization, we want to know about it. Your job will be to infiltrate the Oklahoma City chapter and discover if they are planning to attack SAC installations in that state."

"What's SAC?" Remo asked.

"Strategic Air Command," Smith said.

"Oh. Why Oklahoma City?" Remo wanted to know.

"Our computers worked out a high probability that if there is an unaccounted member of that group, and that person took off with the FOES van, he would probably have taken Route 40 out of the state and into Oklahoma, probably going to the nearest large city, which is

Oklahoma City, where there is another chapter of FOES. The nearest one to Little Rock, incidentally.''

''And suppose these loonies want to go eat our missiles or something?'' Remo asked.

''You will disband that chapter permanently,'' Smith said coldly.

''Why don't you just come out and say, 'You will kill them to the last man'?''

''Because you said it for me. I'll leave an information package on UFOs so you can pass yourself off as an interested believer. And I'll speak to Chiun if I see him. About those fingernails.''

''And suppose this group comes up clean?'' Remo asked.

''Go on to the next one. They have chapters throughout the country, but most of them are in the Midwest—which is where our largest concentrations of defensive missiles are.''

''Great,'' said Remo. ''Just what I've always wanted. To go on a nationwide nut chase. Sure I shouldn't grow my fingernails first?''

''Good day, Remo.''

''Yeah, yeah. Well, at least I'll be able to leave this stupid city. Maryland is the only place in the country where they laid down the Mason-Dixon Line when they were drunk. The west half thinks it belongs to the north and the east is still waiting for the south to rise again.''

But Smith wasn't listening. He had already gone.

When Chiun returned, he was no longer not speaking to Remo.

''Emperor Smith has gone mad again,'' he declared loudly.

''He explained how the fingernails would endanger the operation?''

''He said something of the sort. But I ignored him because he was obviously raving. He is sending us on some personal vendetta against throwers of whizzbees.''

"Against what?"

"Whizzbee throwers. You know, Remo. You have seen them. In parks, on streets. There must be thousands of them, hundreds in this dirty city alone. They work in twos, throwing ugly plastic whizzbees back and forth. As a game."

"Oh, you mean Frisbees," Remo said.

"Yes, whizzbees. We are to exterminate all throwers of whizzbees in your country. Because they missed, Emperor Smith said. It makes no sense to me. The man is mad," finished Chiun, who always called Smith "Emperor" because the House of Sinanju had worked for emperors since the Pharaohs. Even though times had changed and Smith chose to call himself a director, because Sinanju worked for him, Smith was thereby exalted by the association with Sinanju and would forevermore be known as Emperor. At least in the annals of Sinanju.

"No, you've got it wrong, Chiun," Remo corrected. "Smith doesn't want us to hit Frisbee players. He wants us to go after some flying saucer people."

"Flying saucers? Whizzbees? Are they not the same thing? They are flat and they fly when thrown."

"No, flying saucers are different. They don't exist—I don't think . . ."

Chiun stopped gesticulating and regarded Remo steadily with narrowed hazel eyes. "Aah. Now it is clear. Now you are the mad one, Remo. You accepted a contract to go after people who don't exist."

"No, Chiun. It's—look, never mind. I'll explain it another time. It's too complicated. We've got to pack."

"You pack. I am busy."

"Doing what?" Remo asked.

"I am busy," Chiun repeated and turned his back toward Remo. Remo could see he was fiddling with his kimono.

A minute later, Chiun turned around and with a broad

smile said, "Here, Remo. I have brought something for you."

"Yeah? What?" Remo asked suspiciously.

"It is a toy. A very simple toy. Many American children play with them, and I have one for you to try."

Remo looked at the multicolored block in Chiun's delicate hands and said, "That's no toy. That's a Rubik's Cube. You've got to be a mathematical genius to line those little squares up right."

"Nonsense," said Chiun. "It is a simple toy. The child who gave me this was himself proficient in its use."

"What child?"

"The one who gave this to me. The one I just spoke about," Chiun said logically.

"Why would a child give you his Rubik's Cube?" demanded Remo.

"Because he dared me to solve it, and I said I would only solve this toy if the toy were the reward for my effort. Masters of Sinanju do not put forth effort without compensation."

"You took that thing away from a kid? I'm ashamed of you, Chiun."

"I did not take it. I earned it," Chiun sniffed.

"Wait a minute. You solved that thing? All by yourself?"

"Of course," Chiun said blandly. "I am the Master of Sinanju."

"I don't believe it. Prove it."

Chiun, taken aback, hesitated and then said stiffly, "Very well, Remo. I will show you." He gathered the cube close to him, holding it with both hands and bent his ancient head. As Remo bent forward for a closer look, Chiun's frail-seeming hands became a blur.

"See, Remo," crowed Chiun, holding the cube up. Each side was a solid color.

"I didn't see your hands," Remo said.

"You saw the cube. You saw me hold the cube. Then

you saw me raise the cube and the cube was correctly done. What more is there to see?"

"You might have had another cube stashed in your clothes and switched them."

"Really, Remo. I would not stoop to such subterfuge."

"But you would stoop to conning a little kid."

"I have taught the child a valuable lesson. Not to speak with strangers." Chiun suddenly perked up. "Here, now you try."

Remo took the cube. Chiun had twisted it again, so the little colored squares were in a haphazard pattern. Remo knew, because he had read it somewhere, that there were a quintillion or more possible hand-moves and combinations of arrangements of the mobile squares, and only someone who knew the exact moves necessary to align the squares properly could solve the puzzle. Most people gave up, not understanding that it couldn't be accomplished by trial and error, like a jigsaw puzzle. On the other hand, proficient people could solve the cube in under a minute.

Remo had just seen Chiun do it in about six seconds. Even with Chiun's superhuman reflexes and coordination, it didn't make sense that Chiun, who knew no more about higher mathematics than he did about baseball, could master the puzzle so quickly.

Remo spent five minutes trying, and all he managed was to get a bunch of blue squares in an L shape on one side, and a cluster of orange ones on the other. There was a blue square in the middle of the orange cluster, and when Remo tried to get that onto the right side, he lost the orange cluster. Then he gave up.

"Heh, heh, heh," cackled Chiun. "Short attention span. I was right."

"Right about what?" Remo fumed.

"Right that you are not ready to master the art of the Killing Nail. Anyone who cannot solve a child's puzzle is not prepared mentally for the later stages of Sinanju."

And having absolved himself of his earlier misjudgment, Chiun, the reigning Master of Sinanju, repaired to the kitchenette to make breakfast.

Remo decided he wasn't hungry.

CHAPTER FIVE

Remo Williams read about flying saucers on the flight to Oklahoma City. Smith's information package consisted of raw data in the form of newspaper clippings, magazine articles, Air Force studies, case histories and computer printouts from CURE. If the CURE computer ever processed this hodgepodge of facts, reports, statistics and wild speculations into a concrete evaluation, Smith had neglected to provide the results.

For once, Remo was not bothered by Chiun. In fact, Chiun was barely in his seat for most of the flight—the one that he always took so he would be the first to know if the wings fell off—and instead walked up and down the aisles, happily demonstrating his ability with Rubik's Cube to anyone who cared to watch. Remo still couldn't figure out how Chiun did it, and it aggravated him.

In Oklahoma City, they registered in a hotel near the Will Rogers World Airport. Remo signed the register as Remo Greeley, the cover name Smith had given him. He was supposed to be a freelance writer affiliated with a tabloid that ran a lot of UFO articles, here in Oklahoma City to do an article on FOES. Remo turned to ask Chiun if he wanted to sign in, but Chiun was off by the elevators, where he had collected a group of bellboys, who stared wide-eyed at Chiun's cube-solving speed.

With a perverse grin, Remo signed the book for Chiun, writing on it, "Hen Nee Yung Man." Chiun would never know.

By afternoon, Remo had read most of the UFO material. He learned that since 1947, when a pilot sighted a formation of plate-shaped objects flying over a mountain range in Washington State and coined the term "flying saucer," UFO sightings had been occurring regularly with only periodic fluctuations. Most of these sightings, about 95.7 percent, according to Folcroft computers, were the result of unskilled people mistaking airplane lights, observation balloons, meteorites and other natural phenomena. The remaining 4.3 percent were simply unidentified. They could be anything—even spacecraft from beyond the earth.

This last was a possibility, according to one set of statistics, which claimed that there were so many stars in the sky that if only one in a billion of them shone on a planet that harbored intelligent life, then mathematically speaking there would be millions of inhabited worlds in the universe. Remo didn't buy it. Even if the numbers were true, nothing said that these intelligent beings could build interstellar spaceships, or that they would bother to visit Earth, even if they could in less than a hundred million zillion years. Or that these beings, no matter how intelligent, might not be exactly human and therefore might not be able to build a treehouse, never mind a spaceship. You had to have hands to build something, right? Remo wondered idly if some of them might not look like Rubik's Cubes. If they did, then the invasion had already begun and all bets were off. They had already gotten to Chiun.

Reading through the eyewitness accounts of reported contact with aliens, Remo learned that UFOs came from the planet Venus and were piloted by tall, long-haired friendly Venusians; that they also came from Mars and were built by short, hairy, vicious creatures intent upon kidnaping South American women for sexual gratification; that they were the work of an underground supercivilization from within the earth itself, who flew out of an unknown hole in the North Pole; or that they were scientific probes from a distant star and manned by gray-skinned vivisectionists with no lips and eyes like tomcats.

Every report contradicted every other one. Except that most of them quoted the aliens as being very concerned about our atomic weapons. And that was why they were here. To make sure it didn't get out of hand.

That was the only common denominator. And the only factor that fit in with the attack on the missile site.

There was a file on FOES, which insisted that the letters stood for Flying Object Evaluation Center, proving to Remo that Smith's computers weren't always infallible. FOES had been founded in 1953 in Dayton, Ohio, and over the years had sprouted chapters in several states. The only unusual activity associated with any chapter took place only a couple of years ago, when a chapter in Utah tried to force the Central Intelligence Agency to make its top-secret files on UFOs open to public inspection under the Freedom of Information Act. The case had gone all the way to the Supreme Court, which threw the suit out when the CIA convinced the Court that it had already released 99 percent of all its data and the remaining data contained the names of agents who might be compromised. A representative of FOES was later quoted as saying that national security should never stand in the way of the pursuit of truth, and said that this "only proved that the UFO cover-up carried on by the government since the forties stretched all the way to the Supreme Court."

"What are you reading?" Chiun asked at one point.

"Confusion," Remo said, and threw Smith's files into the wastebasket.

"From Emperor Smith, of course," said Chiun, who then dropped the subject. "Is Cheeta Ching to be found in this area?" he asked, changing the channels on the television.

"No. Not in Oklahoma."

"Then I will watch my beautiful dramas," Chiun decided, and began setting up the tape system on which he had recorded such soap operas as "As the Planet Revolves" and "The Young and the Wanton," all originally broadcast before sex and violence—overt sex and violence, anyway—invaded daytime television.

Knowing that this would keep Chiun occupied well into the early evening, Remo decided to leave him and infiltrate the local FOES chapter on his own. Chiun would only complicate Remo's carefully thought-out plan—which Remo had yet to devise. Regardless of what it turned out to be, though, he knew Chiun would complicate it. Besides, he was getting sick of that stupid cube.

"I'm going out, Chiun. Don't wait up."

But Chiun made no sign that he heard, already being immersed in the sad story of Dr. Lawrence Walters, psychiatrist at large, who had just learned from Betty Hendon that her husband, the insane billionaire Wilfred Wyatt Hornsby, whom she had married when only a teenager, was planning a sex change operation so he could marry Betty's father, who had been posing as Betty's mother and as the upstairs maid in the house of Jeremy Bladford, the man she truly loved.

Remo closed the door of the bedroom as he picked up his dark blue nylon windbreaker, which he put over his black T-shirt and chinos. The phone in the bedroom gave him his plan. Screw this freelance writer crap, he thought, and dropped the windbreaker, which was only a prop.

Remo dialed the number of the local FOES chapter. Normally, Remo could never remember phone numbers, but this one he had just read in the files, and it had the same exchange as the hotel. The rest of the dial sequence was FOES. That, Remo could remember. So he dialed the exchange of the hotel phone and F-O-E-S.

"Flying Object Evaluation Center," a twangy female voice said.

"Hi," Remo said. "My name is Remo Greeley. I want to report a UFO."

"Really? In this area?" The woman's voice rose a full octave and skittered dangerously close to a falsetto.

"Yeah. This area. Just outside of town," Remo said in a bored voice. "Saw it just ten minutes ago."

"Where, where? What did it look like?" the woman squealed. Then, catching herself, she asked calmly, "If you could give us the exact time, place, and circumstances and describe the object as best as you can in your own words, please. This conversation is being recorded."

"Right. Okay, here goes." Remo heard a tape recorder's beep and searched his mind for a description, trying to remember if the Martians were the tall hippies or the hairy, apelike creatures. "It was shaped like a penguin, about four feet tall—"

"The UFO was shaped like a penguin?"

"No, no. The guy who came out of the UFO and talked to me was shaped like a penguin. The spaceship was kinda like a bowl with a blue bubble on top. Or was it on the bottom?" Remo couldn't keep the various classifications of UFO shapes straight, either. He knew that most flying saucers were not shaped like saucers at all, but like spheres, eggs, cigars or just bright lights.

"You had a Close Encounter of the Third Kind?" the woman screeched, hurting Remo's eardrum. "Hey, Ralph, get on the extension. I have someone who's made contact. . . . Go ahead, Mr. Green."

"Greeley. Remo Greeley. I was driving along and my car stopped in the middle of the road without any reason. Then this bright thing came down and lighted up the road."

"I thought you said this happened just ten minutes ago," the woman asked suspiciously.

"Yeah, ten minutes ago."

"How could it light up the road in broad daylight? It's three o'clock in the afternoon."

"Um, these were very, very bright lights. The penguin explained to me that they were brand new."

"What else did he say?"

"He was upset. Very upset. He said that he wanted the world to stop building atomic weapons and things. Said it endangered the penguins of the universe. I guess it was like Save the Whales or something. He even gave me a button, but I can't read it. Anyway, he said it's got to stop."

"Yeah, they all say that," the woman breathed. "All the reports we get agree on that one point for some reason. Did this creature say where he was from?"

"From?"

"Yes, he had to be from somewhere, didn't he? I mean, in order to get here he obviously had to come from somewhere else."

"Right. Oh, right. I get you now. As a matter of fact he said he was from the Milky Way."

"Sir," the woman said steadily. "The Milky Way is not a place. It's a cluster of stars, each of which is millions of miles apart. Our sun is one of those stars, so when you're talking about the Milky Way, you're talking about quite a bit of territory."

Damn, thought Remo. He should have known that. "Well, I can't help that. It's what the little guy told me. I mean, if he doesn't know where he's from, who does?"

"You've got a point there. Maybe he just didn't want to leave an address. He's not still there, is he?"

"No, but he said he might be back."

"In that case, he may try to contact you again. It would be best if you were to come over to our headquarters and give a full description to our staff. Could you do that?"

"Okay. I'll be right over," said Remo.

"That's Suite Fifteen, the Stigman Building. We'll be here. Oh, goodie," she said just before Remo hung up on her.

"Moron," Remo muttered.

The Stigman building was only a few blocks away, so

Remo walked, enjoying the cool air and wishing Smitty hadn't given him this dippy assignment.

"Oh, you must be Remo Greeley," a frizzy-haired red-head said to Remo when he walked into the headquarters of FOES. "This is really exciting. Now you're both here."

"Both?" Remo said.

"That's right. After you called, Ms. Bull showed up. She saw the UFO, too. Isn't that exciting? And she said it's still there."

"She did? Still where?" Remo wondered if he'd screwed up the description and they were playing a joke to get back at him.

"Still in the woods down in Chickasha. Oh, it's so exciting," the woman said. Remo decided that her hair wasn't red, but more of an orange color, and that while she looked a roly-poly 36, she was probably a plump 24 years old tops. She wore a lot of rings and bangles, none of which helped. She was the receptionist Remo had talked to before.

"We're all about to drive out there now," she burbled, bouncing to her feet. "You're coming, of course."

"Of course," Remo said. He didn't understand what was going on, but whatever it was, it would make his job of keeping tabs on these loonies easier.

"Is everyone ready?" a blonde as tall and slim as a birch tree asked as she led a contingent of people out into the reception room where Remo was. "Oh, who are you?" she asked him, when her cool gray eyes alighted on him.

"This is Mr. Greeley," the receptionist said. "He saw the same object you did. But he describes it a little differently."

"Yeah, mine had a penguin," Remo said.

"I see . . ." the blonde said slowly, looking Remo up and down, which caused Remo to wonder if his fly was open. "My name is Amanda Bull. Are you a member of FOES, Mr. Greeley?"

"Call me Remo. No, but I'm thinking of joining."

"I see," she said again. "Well, you better come with us then, even though you're obviously one of those macho types, which I can't stand."

"I eat quiche," Remo said, wondering what it was that made her say that.

They drove in a van south along a big highway flanked by flat farmland. The van that was customized so that the outside depicted scenes of various close encounters, and the inside was perfect for viewing the skies because of a bubble roof hatch.

"Gee," the orange-haired FOES receptionist remarked as Amanda drove. "This would make a swell official van for our group."

Amanda said nothing. She had been trying to draw Remo out on his close encounter, but Remo gave so many evasive answers, she gave up after a while.

Remo, out of boredom, looked out the window for something to occupy his mind. There were no telephone poles to count. He tried counting cows, but the third farm they passed had about fifty of them packed close together, and Remo decided to forget it. The only interesting part of the trip was when they passed over first a big river and then a little river.

It was twilight when Amanda pulled over and said, "Here. This is the spot. Everybody out."

Then Amanda Bull stepped out, dressed in a sky-blue jumpsuit that made her willowy body look inviting even to Remo, to whom sex was no longer a mystery and for whom women, as a consequence, weren't even important enough to him to be sex objects anymore. And she took firm control of the seven people who made up the Oklahoma City chapter of FOES.

"We'll march, single file, after me. I have a flashlight, so keep your eyes on my light. The spacecraft is in these woods. Let's go. March."

Remo fell in behind Amanda Bull, and the others straggled in back of him, chattering like monkeys.

"Ever been in the army?" Remo asked Amanda.

"No, why do you ask?" she said.

"Oh, nothing. It's just that the last time I heard anyone give orders like you, it was my Marine drill instructor back in boot camp."

Amanda grunted. "I knew you were the macho type. Vietnam?"

"Someplace like that," Remo said.

"Well, you'd better be receptive to change because none of that military stuff is going to last much longer."

"I thought we were just out here on a flying saucer hunt," suggested Remo, who thought it was interesting that this woman, who hated the military, acted as though she belonged to an army herself.

"You'll see. Now keep quiet. Everybody. We're getting close."

Remo thought he was getting close, too. Amanda Bull, if that was her name, didn't act or dress or talk like any of the other UFO collectors—or whatever they were. Where the others didn't seem to be wrapped at all, the blonde was wrapped *too* tight. And she had a crummy personality. Frustration, Remo decided. Maybe he would have to remedy that, he thought with absolutely no enthusiasm whatsoever.

They came to a clearing. Just beyond the glow of Amanda's flashlight was a dark shape that glittered a little. Without a word, Amanda broke away from the group and got in front of the dark shape.

"*Behold,*" she shouted triumphantly. "*The emissary of a new age!*"

Light flooded the clearing. It was mostly white light, like calcium set on fire, but there were smaller blue and red and green lights mixed in with the overpowering white ones, and they illuminated the tall form of Amanda Bull, her arms raised as if she were Caesar before his armies.

"My God," the frizzy-haired FOES receptionist gasped, "it's just like the movie." Her name was Ethel

Sump, and she had seen *Close Encounters of the Third Kind* sixteen times, seventeen if you counted the time she sat through it four times in one evening and fell asleep midway through the midnight showing, only to wake up on the floor of the deserted theater the next morning to the sound of her dry popcorn belch.

The others froze where they were, the light etching expressions of amazement on their open faces.

Remo dropped flat and shut his eyes until he could close down the sensitive pupils of his eyes and not be blinded by the light.

He listened.

"Citizens of Earth," Amanda called. "I am the chosen representative of the new Earth, an Earth in which war and pestilence and sexism will be no more. From the distant star Betelgeuse comes the mighty World Master, architect of the golden age that is about to dawn. He has entrusted me with the task of recruiting preparation groups through which his teachings will enable Earth's glorious destiny to be fulfilled." Amanda paused to catch her breath, then said, "We ask you to join us now."

The speech had a remarkable effect on the members of FOES. It went right over their heads.

"Huh? What's she talking about?" someone demanded, squinting through the light.

"Something about improving the world," Ethel Sump said. "I don't see the penguin. Where's the penguin, Mr. Greeley?"

But Remo had already rolled into the trees and was on his feet running. He moved through the trees, circling to get around behind the lights. He was disturbed by the sudden appearance of those lights from something as big and powerful as this ship or whatever it was. Machinery, especially big machinery, always sent out vibrations. But Remo had picked up nothing like that.

Remo could see that the object was not sitting on the ground, but floated perhaps a yard or so above it. He sensed no engines or motors, felt no flow of air to indicate fans or jets or any other type of motive force. Just the heat of high-intensity lights and a blankness where there should have been vibration.

It was eerie and unsettling. Remo didn't even sense much mass, even though the object was bigger than a bus and made of some silvery metal, if its polished surface was any indication.

There should at least have been mass, he thought, if not vibration. Instead, Remo felt emptiness or hollowness, as if the UFO were almost completely weightless, or if it could somehow suspend gravity.

Remo got behind the object unseen. The lights were just as strong there, too. So Remo shut out the glare by pinching his lids down, and drifted closer to the thing, whatever it was.

Still no vibration.

With his hands extended Remo touched the hull of the floating object. It gave way slightly before his delicate touch, like a beach ball touched by a swimming child.

Remo's sensitive fingers felt vibration now. Electrical activity. But still nothing like what he would expect of a floating monster like this. Maybe it ran on batteries. How many size D batteries would it take to power a ship across deep space? Remo didn't know. What happened when the batteries went dead? Did they stop at the intergalactic grocery store and buy more? He put his fingers on the fabric of the space ship, ready to tear it open, when suddenly a thin, reedy voice emanated from inside the cool skin of the UFO and said, *"Preparation Group Leader. An unauthorized person has ventured too close to my craft. Retreat a distance of fifty meters, please."*

"Everybody run," Amanda Bull yelled, her voice shocked. And she and the FOES group all ran as a deep humming grew in pitch; at the same time the lights all over the object dimmed in inverse ratio to the humming.

Under his fingers, Remo felt the vibrations intensify.

He decided to back off until he found what the humming was, but as he ran, the humming seemed to follow him. Or something did, because his skin became hot. There was a warmth under his clothes, which turned into a burning sensation, especially in the places where his clothes were tight, in the backs of the knees, down the back, and even in his feet.

While he was running he glanced back. The UFO floated into the sky and, its lights extinguished, vanished past the treetops. At the same time the sound of the FOES van leaving the scene rapidly came to his ears.

Only when they were both gone did the burning stop. But Remo had already collapsed. And he couldn't explain why.

CHAPTER SIX

The first time the telephone rang, the Master of Sinanju ignored it. He was engrossed in his beautiful dramas. Not that Chiun would have deigned answer the insistent ringing even if he were not already occupied. The Master of Sinanju was not a servant. He did not answer telephones, which invariably rang because some inconsiderate and unimportant fat white person wished to speak with Remo and was too lazy to write a letter or appear in person, which were the only proper ways to communicate with someone. Usually the calls were from Emperor Smith, which made no difference to Chiun. Just because the Master of Sinanju treated Smith like an emperor, it did not mean that Chiun liked Smith or took his calls. Just his gold.

The second time the phone rang, there were commercials coming over the Betamax, and Chiun quickly went to the phone, knowing that he had exactly 180 seconds to handle the interruption.

At first, Chiun was merely going to crush the receiver into dust, which he knew from past experience would permanently silence the device. But this usually caused Remo to complain, except when Remo was unhappy with Smith, in which case Remo might crush the phone himself. In deference to his pupil, Chiun caught a loop of phone wire and, with an upward swipe of a single long-nailed finger, neatly severed the cord. If Remo complained later, Chiun would point to the cut cord as an excellent example of the art of the Killing Nail, which would probably silence Remo.

The Master of Sinanju returned to the Betamax just in time to catch the climax of "As the Planet Revolves" and Julie's shocking admission of her kleptomania.

Five minutes later, the Betamax stopped dead.

Chiun's wispy beard and hair trembled slightly, and his hazel eyes turned to slits. This had never before happened. Had the stupid machine broken? It was a gift from Smith and therefore the handiwork of whites, and subject to difficulties as all white things were. Chiun got up to examine the device.

There was a knock at the door. A timid knock. Then a small voice called through the panel, "Mr. Yung Man? Sorry about the electricity. I was told that I should give you a message from your son. He said to cut the electricity first because you never answered the phone and might be watching television, in which case you'd never hear me knock because of your hearing problem . . ."

"Go away, idiot," Chiun called. "You have the wrong person. You are speaking to the Master of Sinanju, who can hear a blade of grass grow outside his window. Begone."

"But your son, Remo, asked me to give you a message."

The startled hotel manager suddenly found himself staring into a wrinkled face where he could have sworn a closed veneer door had stood only a second before. There was a door, then there was no door, just the old Oriental in the silk bathrobe. But no sound or motion of the opening of the door.

"Where is my son?" demanded the old Oriental. "What message does he send?"

"He—he's sick. He's at a phone booth next to a Burger Triumph stand on the main highway leading to Chickasha, just south of here. He said you should come right away."

"Begone and call me a taxi car. I will be down shortly.

And I will expect my machine to be working again when I return.''

The cabby had had stranger fares before—he thought. First there was this old Chinese character who came flying out of the hotel and as he bounded into the back seat, cried, ''My son is ill, and you will take me to him instantly. I will pay you well for your speed.''

''Okay, feller. Where is he?'' He got the cab rolling.

''He is at a telephone, beside a place where they cook those disgusting meat things you creatures are always consuming.''

''Say what?'' asked the driver, who wondered what he'd landed by way of a fare.

''A burger thing.''

''Oh, Burger Triumph. But which one? There's millions of 'em around these parts.''

''The one on the road leading to Chickentown, due south.''

''Chick—oh, Chickasha! That's good enough. We'll find him.''

They found Remo seated with his back to a telephone booth. In front of him stood a huge roadside rubbish can overflowing with Burger Triumph wrappers, paper cups, and half-eaten cheeseburgers.

''*Aiiee*.'' The Master of Sinanju screamed when the cab pulled up to the booth and he beheld Remo semiconscious amid the litter.

Remo looked up with glazed eyes. Oddly, the glassiness made them look more alive than usual. He had seen so much death that it was as if his eyes had absorbed it.

''Little Father . . .'' Remo mumbled. ''I tried to get you by phone . . .''

''Never mind,'' Chiun snapped, looking from Remo to the overstuffed barrel. ''You have outdone yourself this time, Remo.''

"What's up? What's the matter with him?" the cabby asked.

"He has slipped back into utter degradation," Chiun said.

"Yeah, I can see that. Booze?"

"Worse."

"Worse?"

"Yes, he has gorged himself on filth. Forgetful of his heritage, he has reverted to whiteness."

"He does look kind of pale at that. If he's your son, that's pretty bad."

"He is not my son. He is a filthy white meat-eater who has violated centuries of tradition. And for what? For hamburgers. Remo, you must have eaten over a hundred hamburgers." Chiun's strident voice lapsed into puzzled plaintiveness. "Why, Remo? I thought you had passed that disgusting phase." Truthfully, this behavior made no sense. As part of his Sinanju training, Remo had long ago given up beef, and an unfortunate incident years ago in which he had almost died from eating a hamburger his metabolism was unable to accept cured him of any relapses to his pre-Sinanju days. In fact, Remo should be dead now, if those hamburger wrappings were any indication of his most recent meal.

"I am waiting for an explanation, Remo," Chiun said sternly.

"Not burgers," Remo mumbled thickly. "Arms and legs. Look."

"What?" Chiun asked.

"He said look at his arms and legs," the cabby said helpfully.

"I know what he said, white. Return to your car."

Chiun bent down and rolled back one of Remo's pants legs and saw the redness of the skin, which contrasted to the paleness of Remo's bare arms and face and made him resemble a comic-book Indian.

"These are burns, Remo."

"Right. Burns. Whole body burned."

"Your arms are not burned. Nor is your face." Chiun examined Remo's other leg. The skin was seared. Not deeply, but thoroughly—although in some places the redness was lighter. The hairs on Remo's legs were not singed, which was strange. Remo's chest was burned also.

Examining Remo's arms, Chiun found that the upper biceps were seared, but only those parts above the short sleeves of his T-shirt. Below, the skin was unaffected. The burns might have been abnormally severe sunburns, except that the exposed parts of Remo's body, which logically would be the ones to experience sunburn, were normal. It was just the opposite.

Chiun, who had lived more than 80 years and had confronted nothing he could not understand, felt something like a chill run along his spine.

"How were you burned, Remo?" the Master of Sinanju said urgently. "What did this to you?"

"Lights. Pretty lights. Shiny. Burns."

Then Remo's head fell forward as he collapsed. Chiun scooped him up into his arms as if Remo were a baby.

"Quickly," Chiun called back to the driver. "We must get him back to the hotel."

"Let me give you a hand, old timer," the driver started to say, but before he could move, the old Oriental straightened up with Remo held tenderly in his arms, and carried him back to the cab without any effort at all.

"I'm not gonna ask how you did that," the cabby said into the rearview mirror as he drove back to Oklahoma City.

"And I am not going to tell you," Chiun said as he ministered to Remo in the back seat.

"I don't understand what it is you are saying, Chiun," Dr. Harold W. Smith was saying through the new telephone Chiun had demanded be installed in his apartment "because some lunatic had ruined the old one."

''Then I will say it again,'' Chiun said across the scrambled line. ''I found my son Remo burned as if by the sun. He is unconscious and cannot tell me what befell him.''

''You called me because Remo has a sunburn?'' demanded Smith with ill-disguised incredulity.

''No, I called you because Remo does not have a sunburn. He does not get sunburned, but if he did, I could deal with it. This sunburn-which-is-not is something new. Something I do not understand. He has one of those education burns.''

''Education burns?'' Smith, in his office overlooking Long Island Sound, hastily gulped two Alka-Seltzer tablets and water. Sometimes he longed for the old days in the CIA without Remo's flip attitude and without Chiun's language barrier.

''Yes, education burns. I have read of them. When a person is burned, the severity of those burns determines his education,'' repeated Chiun, who sometimes longed to be back in Sinanju, without Remo's lack of responsibility or Emperor Smith's inability to communicate in his own language.

''Oh,'' said Smith. ''You mean as in first-, second-, or third-degree burns.''

''Yes. Remo has the least of these. To an ordinary person, this would merely be an inconvenience, but Remo's essence is developed beyond ordinariness. He is now insensible.''

''Will he recover?'' demanded Smith, who knew that if something should happen to Remo, something serious, he would have to order Remo liquidated and then dissolve CURE, finally ending his own life. Chiun, who did not understand that exposure of CURE would be an admission that America did not work and therefore did not understand CURE, would quietly return to his village after he had killed Remo—which would be his task under those circumstances.

''Thanks to my healing skills, he will recover. I will

make him recover whether he wishes to or not. Now he sleeps like a child—the child that he is.''

Smith suppressed a relieved sigh. "That is good. How soon will that be? He is in the middle of an assignment.''

"I know this," Chiun said abruptly. "What I do not know is what he met with which burned the skin beneath his clothes and which did not burn exposed flesh. This you must tell me.''

"Wait one moment. You say his skin is burned. But not as it would be by sunburn, but instead exactly the opposite?''

"Yes. Opposite of reality.''

"Just a minute," Smith said, as he pressed a concealed button on his desk and a hidden desktop computer console rose up. Smith keyed a description of the scientific phenomenon into the files of the computer's memory banks, and then punched in the circumstances Chiun had explained to him. The screen went blank, and the cursor raced across the screen like a spider, leaving behind the greenish words that were the answer Smith needed.

"I have it," Smith said. "Ultrasonics.''

"Speak English," Chiun snapped.

"I said Remo was affected by ultrasonics. Sound pitched to a degree higher than human ears can perceive. This has been worked out to some degree in laboratories and in practical experiments. Focused ultrasonics have the property of creating heat between interfacing surfaces but don't affect surfaces not in contact with other surfaces. It fits exactly. Remo obviously entered an ultrasound field, which caused intense heat between his skin and clothes, enough to create an effect like a severe sunburn. Exposed skin wasn't affected unless it touched something else.''

"Where would Remo have encountered this ultrasonic?''

"I don't know. It must have something to do with his assignment.''

"You told me his assignment had to do with flying whizzbees."

"That's right. Flying saucers are another name for Unidentified Flying Objects. Lights in the sky that people see."

"Lights in the sky? Remo said something about lights."

"Then he must have gotten on to something. He was supposed to infiltrate a group of UFO watchers, FOES."

"Explain to me about these lights."

Smith cleared his throat. "Well, for several years now, people in this country and around the world—but mostly in this country—have seen or thought they've seen peculiar objects in the sky—lights, objects, fires, etc. Most of them are ordinary phenomena like planets and aircraft, but some aren't easily explained. There's a popular theory that these UFOs are ships from other worlds, that they are the work of advanced civilizations who have been monitoring Earth for thousands of years. I find this a bit hard to swallow myself, the idea of advanced civilizations greater than our own—"

"What is so difficult about that?" Chiun said. "I am from an advanced civilization—Korea."

"Yes. Well, uh, Remo's job was to investigate this group to see if they had made contact with an individual calling himself the World Master, who might be influencing them to attack America's missile defense system. Most of this is contained in the files I gave Remo."

"Then this group is responsible for what happened to my son?" Chiun said slowly.

"Possibly. But at this point we must assume that they are probably harmless."

"No one is harmless. Especially the foolish," Chiun said and hung up.

Chiun went over to Remo, whom he had stripped and then washed with special ointments and laid in a bed. Chiun normally discouraged Remo from using a bed, but its soft mattress was the perfect resting place for his injured body. Bending his old head, Chiun listened to Remo's breathing. Its rhythms were returning. Good. Yes, Remo would get better. Most of it was shock, and the shock had triggered defensive sleep mechanisms.

Chiun then retrieved the files Remo had tossed into a wastebasket, and began reading them. As he read, Chiun grew excited. His beard trembled. The more he read, the more agitated he seemed to become. His clear eyes took upon a peculiar, shocked light. Under his breath, Korean words spilled forth. Harsh words at first, then quieter ones. Words of astonishment.

Hours later, when Chiun rose from his lotus position, his parchment face, ordinarily the color of aged ivory, was now more the color of old bone. And there was a strange expression on his face, one that would have puzzled Remo Williams had he been awake to see it. It was the expression of someone who, after a lifetime, has seen a great truth that had previously escaped him.

It was an expression of wonder and joy and a hint of fear.

Chiun returned to Remo's bedside and spoke softly, as if he could hear. "Why did you not tell me of this, my son? Did you not recognize this great thing for what it truly was? Foolish child, you ventured where only the reigning Master of Sinanju has the experience to go. And you have paid the price. But I will make these things right, and I will go forth for the greater glory of Sinanju. You will share in this glory, Remo, when you are well, never fear. But first you must become well. I will return for you when my pilgrimage is over. Good-bye, Remo."

So saying, the Master of Sinanju sat down to write a note with a goose quill, which he left on the dresser beside his sleeping son, and quietly and thoughtfully left the apartment and the hotel.

CHAPTER SEVEN

Pavel Zarnitsa was not in America to spy on Americans.

No, that was the furthest thing from his mind. Pavel Zarnitsa was in America to spy on the Russians who worked for the Soviet airline, *Aeroflot*. Not all of them. Some were simply Russians who worked for *Aeroflot*, and these Russians were no problem. They were civilians.

But some were not civilians. Some belonged to the GRU, the *Glavnoe Razvedyvatelnoe Uprevlenie*, or the Chief Intelligence Directorate of the Soviet General Staff. The GRU was the world's second most powerful intelligence service in the world, after the KGB, or Committee for State Security, for whom Pavel Zarnitsa worked. That the GRU was as Russian as the KGB made no difference to Pavel Zarnitsa or his superiors. The GRU was a rival to the KGB. They were competition. And they liked to use foreign branches of *Aeroflot* as their "fronts."

It was ironic that it was the capitalistic idea of competition that the Kremlin used to keep the KGB and the GRU on their toes. They were given separate operating budgets but overlapping responsibilities, insuring a certain amount of rivalry and bureaucratic infighting between the two services, and virtually no sharing of intelligence. Probably the CIA knew more about GRU agents in *Aeroflot* than he did, thought Pavel ruefully. But he also knew that the CIA did not know the name of the one KGB agent in New York's *Aeroflot* office, namely himself. The KGB was subtle, despite popular depictions of its agents as thick-necked bulls in gray raincoats and fedoras. The GRU was not so subtle. Often, in fact, they were clumsy dolts. Still, they could be effective and had good men—some good men—working for them.

Pavel Zarnitsa knew this because his brother, Chuzhoi, worked for the GRU. Chuzhoi was younger by ten years, just a boy. But an imaginative boy, Pavel knew, too imaginative for the GRU. Pavel had told him that when Chuzhoi announced his decision not to follow his older brother's footsteps. But Chuzhoi, young and brash like his dead mother, did not listen. He never listened. And so Chuzhoi had gone his way and Pavel his own.

Pavel had seen his brother only once after that. It happened when they were accidentally seated together in a Moscow cafe, where lone diners were always seated with strangers because space was at a premium even at the worst places.

"The stupid capitalists are doomed," Chuzhoi had announced boastfully after Pavel asked how he was doing. "Within five years we will have military parity with them, thanks to their own lax security, and then the inevitable Communist revolution will cover the globe."

"They are not stupid, and no one believes in the glorious revolution anymore, Chuz," Pavel had replied as the two-hour wait for a waitress dragged past. Normally, it would have been a three-hour wait, but the Zarnitsa brothers had clout.

"The democracies are crumbling," Chuzhoi repeated.

Pavel sighed. "Is this what you have learned among the ham-handed GRU?" He felt sad. Most Russians outgrew such talk after they left the Young Communist League. It was indoctrination, nothing more. Pavel tried to explain geopolitical reality to his brother, to explain to him that even as an enemy, America was a friend to Russia.

"We need them. The Americans keep the Chinese in check. Without America, China might attack us. Even the Politburo knows this."

"You have been watching that television program again," Chuzhoi laughed, referring to a popular Russian show that every week televised the adventures of KGB agents fighting black marketeers, traitors and CIA agents in the Soviet Union. The GRU had always resented the fact that the KGB had its own television program and were public heroes, just as the FBI had been the heroes of the Americans until recently. But there was a good reason that there was no GRU program. Average Russians were not told of the GRU's existence.

Pavel shrugged off the suggestion. Sometimes Chuzhoi could be obtuse, and perhaps he belonged in the GRU after all. So he changed the subject and they talked of their boyhood in Kirovograd, in the Ukraine.

Since that chance meeting, the brothers drifted further apart. The last Pavel had heard of him, Chuzhoi was hard at work in one of the GRU's gadget-making factories. Another childish GRU fetish.

Then Pavel had been assigned to infiltrate *Aeroflot*'s New York office to root out and expose GRU operatives when the GRU got the better of the KGB in a budget crunch.

Pavel Zarnitsa discovered that America was wonderful. He loved America. Unlike some, he did not love America because it was so much better than Russia. No, Pavel Zarnitsa was not that kind of Russian. He loved America because it was so much like Russia. It was like coming home to a place that he had forgotten from his youth, so that it was hauntingly familiar and new at the same time.

Oddly, this revelation disturbed Pavel. And he redefined his geopolitical theories.

America and Russia were on an inevitable collision course, Pavel decided. It wasn't because of the differences between the two countries. Actually, it was their similarities that were the problem. Just the reverse of what his brother believed.

Both America and Russia were large industrial nations whose frontiers had been wrested from hostile barbarians by Europeans or Slavs. The Americans had their Indians and the Russians their Mongols and Tatars. One country's redskin was the other's yellowskin.

In time both nations filled out their natural boundaries and sought to expand beyond them. In America, it was the acquisition of new states and territories, like Alaska and Guam. With Russia, it had been the Ukraine and Byelorussia, then client states, most of which had been acquired after World War II. Then these client states had been brought into line only to act as a buffer against the dangerous western part of Europe, which had always been war prone and would always be war prone.

And then there were the Asians. Huge China and its hungry masses. China would always be a problem, even a Communist China. Especially a Communist China.

America, which had more or less friendly neighbor countries and nothing but ocean to the east and west, never understood that.

Could Russia be blamed for entering the war against Japan only after the Nazis had fallen, and only two days after the atomic bomb had been dropped on Hiroshima, (thus insuring victory for the Allies), even if all Russia did was enter the northern part of Japanese-held Korea and fire a few rounds? When, less than a month later, the Japanese surrendered, Russia, technically one of the victorious occupying armies, swallowed up half of Korea.

Shrewd. But that was the Russian way. America was shrewd, too. Perhaps not quite as shrewd, but Americans were canny. Hadn't they acquired Alaska from us in such a way that it at first seemed as if America had the worst of the deal? An admirable people. Just like the Russians.

Which is why Russia would one day have to crush

America. There was no room for two identical superpowers on this planet. It had been this way back in the beginning of the War—for Russia, there was only one War, World War II—with Stalin and Hitler. They were too much alike, shared too many similar goals. Allies at first, they had split, not over their differences, but over the recognition that only one of them could achieve the goal both sought. If only Americans were more like the Chinese, Pavel thought, it would be different. A war could be fought over differences, settled, and business would revert to normal.

But America was not China. It was another Russia—big, sprawling, ingenious, and hearty. Pavel knew, too, that the only thing worse would be a Communist America. Here was the flaw in his brother Chuzhoi's view. From close observation, Pavel recognized that if any country could make Communism work, it would be the United States. Americans were that way. And if that ever happened, the few differences between the two great superpowers would evaporate, and so would the things that allowed them to coexist. If Americans proved themselves to be better Communists than the Russians, the Soviets could never tolerate that. The two nations would come together like mighty lodestones, bringing destruction to both, and possibly to the world.

But that ultimate conflict could be avoided, Pavel knew. Russia could secretly undermine and outlast the United States as a world power before that time. It might not happen for generations, but it was inevitable. Pavel only hoped he would not see that day, because it would be a sad one. He really liked America. It had everything Russia had, and more of it. And one thing Russia did not have.

Tacos.

There was no food like the taco in all of Russia.

Pavel Zarnitsa had discovered tacos during his first week in New York. He had resolved to sample the food of every restaurant in a widening spiral around his apartment building until he had found a dozen or so in which he could regularly dine. Pavel liked his food, and restaurant eating. With the exception of a Chinese restaurant, which Pavel refused to enter, Pavel found American restaurants to be quite good. He could not believe the fast service, and had to learn to wait until he was actually hungry before going in, not two or three hours before he expected to be hungry, as he had to do in Russia. But when he entered a dingy establishment called the Whacko Taco, Pavel forgot all about all the others.

Pavel didn't even know what a taco was, but it was the cheapest item on the menu, so he ordered two.

When they arrived, looking as limp as uncooked fish, he didn't even know how to eat one. He had to watch other diners until he understood that one didn't use the plastic knife and fork but simply lifted the folded corn tortilla to one's mouth and bit off one end while some of the meat filling dropped out the other end to fall on the plate. This could be eaten with a fork later.

That first taco had been interesting. But it wasn't until he had wolfed down the second that Pavel experienced the sensation he would later dub, borrowing from American drug slang, the "taco rush."

It began with a hot feeling in the pit of the stomach, which spread outward from the solar plexus and was accompanied by a burning in the mouth and a running of the nose. The brain usually felt clearer and sharper at these times. It was not a meal, it was an experience. From that time on, Pavel Zarnitsa became a taco addict.

Doing research, he discovered that tacos were the perfect food. The folded corn tortilla contained something from most of the major food groups, except fish. For fish, Pavel sometimes added a shrimp for garnish, which he washed down with a dark German lager beer.

To experiment, Pavel tried other Mexican foods. Most of these were made of the same basic ingredients as tacos, except that they were served differently, rolled or flat, but not folded like a taco. Somehow, it was never the same, and Pavel stuck with tacos.

"It must be the design," Pavel said as he picked up his date in front of the downtown Manhattan building that sported a winged hammer and sickle emblem and the name AEROFLOT in Cyrillic letters.

His date was Natalya Tushenka, who was 22 and attractive in a slim-hipped way and who had the glossiest black hair Pavel had ever seen. She had agreed to date him unaware that Pavel was KGB and that she was one of three *Aeroflot* reservation clerks whom he had not in his mind cleared of any GRU affiliation. Tonight he would find out for sure. In his apartment. But not before they dined sumptuously at the Whacko Taco.

"I do not understand, Pavel," Natalya asked, wide-eyed. Her eyes were so blue, they hurt. They were the eyes of an innocent. "How can the design of a—a taco have anything to do with the pleasure obtained from eating such a thing?"

"I do not understand either," admitted the KGB agent. "I only know that somehow it is different with tacos than other food. Like it is different with some women." He gave Natalya a steady glance as they parked near the restaurant.

Natalya laughed like a faraway silver bell. She blushed, too.

And because she blushed, Pavel knew she was GRU, and it saddened him so much that he ate only five tacos that night instead of his usual six. But reality was reality, and no 22-year-old Russian woman who worked for *Aeroflot* would be so innocent as to blush. It was as impossible as a coffee-shop waitress refusing a millionaire's offer of marriage.

At his apartment, Pavel offered Natalya a vodka and a Turkish cigarette, both of which she accepted. He joined her in the vodka, but didn't smoke because he had given her a marijuana cigarette, which she did not realize until she was sufficiently high for him to record her on sound film for his superiors. The vodka ensured that.

When Natalya Tushenka was giggling like a schoolgirl and babbling that she didn't really work for *Aeroflot*, but couldn't say which secret agency she really worked for because it was a secret, silly, Pavel shut off the concealed camera and escorted her down to a taxi and gave the driver instructions to drop her off at the Russian consulate, where her indiscretion would be witnessed by others. The sound film would ensure that she would be dropped from the GRU and returned to Russia in disgrace. Drugs were a serious offense in Russia and unforgivable for an agent.

Because he was unhappy, Pavel Zarnitsa went for a walk, and his feet led him back to the Whacko Taco, where he had that sixth taco he had been unable to eat earlier. After that, he felt better. It was too bad about the girl. But KGB was KGB and GRU was GRU. Besides, she had shown absolutely no appreciation of tacos. She would be happier married and with children, Pavel told himself. And fatter. Definitely fatter. That part made him feel sad all over again.

Before going to bed, Pavel read a late edition, and what he read in that newspaper chased his drowsiness away. There was an item in which the U.S. Air Force officially denied that there had been an accident with a Titan missile in Oklahoma. At the same time the official spokesman denied this, he also denied that another incident had taken place in Arkansas only a few days before. The item was full of words like "alleged" and "unconfirmed" and "sources who wish to remain nameless," and Pavel would not have paid it any attention, but the report was on a back page, in a box and was only three paragraphs long. Therefore he knew it was important. All important news in Russia was printed that way.

Pavel decided that something significant was happening

within America's Strategic Air Command and, whatever it was, he had to find out the truth.

Especially if the Unitted States was going to blow itself up before Pavel Zarnitsa discovered the secret of perfect tacos.

CHAPTER EIGHT

Only two days ago, Ethel Sump had been simply the receptionist for FOES, a group she joined not so much because of her interest in Unidentified Flying Objects, but because belonging to any group made it easier to meet attractive men. At 24, slightly on the plump side, and still unmarried, she knew that time was running out. It was interesting work, even if it didn't pay money, and she got to meet more people than she had at the drive-in pizza place, even if she did miss the $3.70 an hour she was paid at the pizzeria.

Not many dates, though. But Ethel Sump got used to that as her interest in flying saucers grew. After extensive research in UFO magazines and national tabloids, she had arrived at the theory that flying saucers were really from another dimension, which coexisted alongside ours, but which was invisible and intangible until you crossed over into it, and that ghosts, in which she also fervently believed, were really inhabitants of that other dimension and that they became visible only under certain conditions. What those conditions were, Ethel didn't exactly know, but she was sure it had something to do with sunspots.

She was delighted to discover that her theory was correct and to hear it confirmed from the lips—assuming he *had* lips—of that wonderful teacher, the World Master, who had changed her from an ordinary dateless receptionist to an important member of Preparation Group Two, which would carry on the work of Preparation Group One.

"What happened to Preparation Group One?" Ethel had asked when it came her turn to enter the UFO alone. When the group had been called back after the strange incident in the woods, Amanda Bull had invited all FOES members to speak privately with the World Master, who explained in exquisite detail his plans for the planet Earth.

"Preparation Group One has done its work and been rewarded—as you will be," the World Master had said in that funny, high-pitched voice. It was too bad he had to stay hidden behind the glass, but Ethel understood he had to breathe his own air.

Ethel smiled and nodded. She liked rewards. She often gave herself rewards of root beer and Cheeze-its, which were the main contributors to her ungirlish plumpness.

"When the new age dawns, Ethel Sump, you will have a prominent place in it."

"Will I be able to get a date, too?"

"Men will grovel at your feet in the new order."

"I thought you said earlier that we would all be equal then."

"Yes. All men shall grovel at your feet equally. Would you like that, Ethel Sump?"

"Yes, sir. I would."

"Excellent. You understand that my plans necessitate the neutralization of all dangerous weapons on Earth, beginning with nuclear weapons."

"I do," said Ethel Sump, who envisioned herself soon saying "I do" under entirely different circumstances.

"Good," said the figure behind the glass panel. His oversized head reminded Ethel of a tulip bulb moving in a breeze. "And you are prepared to work toward this important goal and obey without question the orders of Group Leader Bull?"

"Sure. But before we do that, can you answer a teeny little question for me?"

"Ask."

"I always thought your people came from another dimension."

"We do."

"But earlier you said you came from—from Betelgeuse."

"Yes, that is true, too," the reedy voice assured her.

"I don't get it. How can they both be true?"

"While my planet does circle that star, in order to traverse the great distances between my world and yours, our ships travel through the Fourth Dimension."

"Oh, I understand now," Ethel Sump beamed.

And when she compared notes with the others and discovered that the World Master had told Marsha Gasse that, yes, his people did come from a subterranean city under the North Pole, and then had informed Martin Cannell that it was true that his people had visited Earth in prehistoric times and created the human race from primeval slime, everyone became puzzled, and they took the matter to Amanda Bull, who was busily organizing the group for the ride back to Oklahoma City.

"Hmmmm," said Amanda, who rubbed the hair on the bridge of her nose in thought. The spaceship was still in the woods, and she briefly considered returning to it to ask the World Master to explain, when she saw the craft rise slowly above the trees and, wobbling, move west. She wondered if the World Master hovered in the atmosphere or had a secret base somewhere.

"The World Master wouldn't lie," Amanda said slowly, which caused the heads of all assembled to nod in agreement. "So they must all be true."

"Why, that makes perfect sense," Martin Cannell said. And that seemed to settle the matter, for they all piled into the van, eager for their first training session.

Ethel Sump enjoyed training, even training with the rifle Amanda gave her, which at first had frightened her. It gave her a sense of purpose and worth. She enjoyed life more in the past two days than in all the years gone before. She even ate less.

Two days of training didn't seem very much, but Amanda had told them all this morning that tonight they would make their first move. The World Master had contacted her somehow and told her so. Amanda had seemed a little worried about that, but as Ethel had reminded her, "The World Master wouldn't let us go out on this important mission unless he knew we were ready," and Amanda said she had to agree.

That would be tonight. But for now, they were pretending to conduct business as usual at FOES headquarters. They were all here, except for that Remo person, who had not been seen since an unauthorized intruder had interrupted their first encounter two nights before. Amanda said that Remo had probably gotten lost in the woods and that he wasn't important because "he was only a man." Ethel didn't see what that had to do with anything; Remo seemed rather attractive. Especially the way he walked. But then, he had claimed to have had a close encounter with a penguin, and nothing had been said about penguins ever since, so maybe Remo didn't matter after all.

So excited was Ethel Sump that she didn't notice the old Oriental gentleman until he had entered the reception area, despite not having been buzzed in.

"Tell whoever is in charge of this place that an important personage has come to see him," said the old man. He couldn't be more than five feet tall or weigh more than 90 pounds, yet he spoke with greater authority than Ethel's old high school principal.

"What important person?" she asked.

"The Master of Sinanju."

"I never heard of you," Ethel said, looking skeptically at the embroidered front of the Oriental's teal blue kimono and wondering if he wasn't one of those cultists looking for a donation.

"I am a personal emissary from your Emperor Smith."

"Emperor Smith? Is he FOES?"

"No, he is friend. He runs your country secretly. I work for him. Defending the Constitution."

"I see," said Ethel, who didn't see at all. "Just a minute." She flicked on the intercom, and in response to Amanda Bull's barked "What is it?" said, "There's an old gentleman here. He seems kind of confused."

"I am not confused, stupid bovine," Chiun snapped. "I am here about the USOs."

"Huh?"

"The lights in the sky. My son, Remo, has seen them."

At the mention of the name Remo over the intercom, Amanda Bull said, "Both of you wait a minute."

"The Master of Sinanju does not wait," Chiun said, and popped the door to Amanda's office off its hinges with a seemingly gentle push of the flat of his hand. The door fell forward, and the Master of Sinanju stepped over it, unconcerned.

"Um . . . how did you do that?" Amanda asked in a tight voice as she came to the doorway.

"With my hand. I am the Master of Sinanju."

"That's right," Ethel put in. "I saw it. He just touched the door and it fell."

Amanda Bull looked at Chiun, then Ethel, and then back at Chiun again as if she suspected them of working together to trick her. Then she remembered that the old Oriental had called Remo Greeley his son, and it was obvious he could not be related to Remo, whom she vaguely suspected of being a spy.

"All right," she said firmly. "Now what's this all about?"

"I am here to make contact," Chiun said flatly, his thin arms folded. "It is important."

"Why?"

"Because it is important to my village. My village knows of these USOs," Chiun said.

"UFOs, not USOs," Amanda corrected.

"I think he wants to join FOES," Ethel whispered. She decided that he might be a confused old man, but he was a likable confused old man.

"No, I want to be friends," Chiun corrected, wondering if all American women were idiots, or just the two in this room.

"Hmmm," Amanda said, pacing the room. The old man might be a spy, too. If he was, the World Master would have to know about this, but Amanda had no way of contacting him except at prearranged times and places.

"If I promise to help you make contact, will you promise to help us tonight?" Amanda asked, thinking about how easily the door had been demolished and how handy that ability might come in tonight.

"Help you with what?"

"We are going on a mission tonight to bring peace to the world."

"A goal many have sought," Chiun said. "How many will *you* kill to achieve it?"

"No violence," Amanda said. "This mission was given us by a being from the UFO. Once this task is done, we will meet with him again. And you may come with us."

"Done," said Chiun. "But first, tell me all about this UFO. What does it look like? Does it bring wisdom?"

"It sure does," put in Ethel Sump. "I've been a better person since I had my first encounter."

"I can see that," said Chiun, watching her plump body jiggle with excitement.

"Come on, then," Amanda ordered, having arranged for the old Chinaman, or whatever he was, to tag along until she could turn him over to the World Master. We've got to get cracking. What did you say your name was?"

"Chiun, reigning Master of Sinanju."

"We'll just call you Chiun for short."

It made no sense to the Master of Sinanju. He, along

with the other members of FOES, which consisted of five
loud women and three untrained men, had journeyed some
distance and were now trudging through an Oklahoma
field where the wheat waved in golden rows under a clear
night sky.

They were on a farm. But they were not here to attack
the farm, the blonde woman with the ugly hair on the
bridge of her nose had informed Chiun. They were here to
destroy something that threatened the peace of the
world. Everyone except Chiun carried weapons, and they
carried them clumsily, as if unfamiliar with their use. They
wore dark clothing and moved like arthritic cats. Amateurs.

"Who has trained you people?" Chiun asked as they
walked.

"Our friend from the UFO," Amanda said.

This seemed to disturb Chiun. "How long have you been
training?"

"Only since two nights ago. Except for me. I've been at
it for about a week."

"Not enough time," Chiun said under his breath.
Aloud, he asked, "And you were provided with these
weapons?"

"No, I got them myself. I wanted to use some of the
weapons the World Master brought with him, but he said
they were too dangerous for humans to use. Too bad. We
could do better work with his disintegrating rays—or
whatever they were."

"You would do better with no weapons at all."

"Are you crazy?" Amanda asked loudly. Then, "There
it is," she hissed. Down, everybody. Let's size up the situation."

Everyone dropped flat except Chiun. In the middle of
the farm, there was a fenced-off rectangle, which appeared
to be empty.

"What is that?" Chiun asked.

"It's a missile silo," Ethel Sump whispered breathlessly. "But how do we get through that fence? It's awful tall."

"How do you think?" said Amanda, digging something out of her backpack. "I brought wire cutters."

"I see no silo," Chiun pointed out.

"That's because it's underground," Amanda said. "See that dark shape? It's the silo cover. The missile is underneath, and somewhere around here is an underground control center. We've got to destroy the missile so it can't fly and kill millions of people."

"Your goal would be better undertaken with worthy tools, not wire cutters and muskets," Chiun said.

Amanda gave Chiun's skinny frame a frosty stare. "I suppose *you* brought some worthy tools with you?"

"Yes," Chiun said, raising his forearms like a surgeon offering his hands to be gloved by a nurse. "Remain here. I will get us through the fence."

"Wait a minute. I'm in charge here!"

But Chiun had already floated off toward the fence. He resembled a silk handkerchief in his blue kimono, one that a strange wind blew along the ground. Chiun drifted first one way, then another, and although all eyes tried to trace his path, he became lost in the darkness long before anyone saw him reach the fence.

Chiun examined the fence. It was of chain link and derived its strength from the interlocked vertical lengths of wire anchored to the four support poles. It could be attacked two ways: by uprooting a pole, which would collapse two sides of the fence, or by attacking any one of the links. Chiun decided upon the latter approach, because it was philosophically purer to destroy a fence through its weak links.

Since he was closer to the bottom than to the top, Chiun worked from the ground up, bringing both hands under the fence edge and grasping two of the interlocks, one in each hand. He brought them together, which placed strain on the rest of the links and released the tension on the links in his hands. As the metal contracted from the lessening of strain, Chiun applied new stress on those relaxed links, more than had been imposed upon them by the normal stress of the fence's structural dynamics.

The fence parted in the middle like an old rag. The two sections sagged forward, and Chiun flitted past, into the former enclosure.

Chiun recognized the radar scoops set on posts for what they were: mere detection devices. They were not a direct threat, so he ignored them.

The silo cover loomed up before him, like a giant childproof cap. The roof was angular and set in twin rails, which ran a short distance off to one side of the cover. Roof and rails were embedded in a tongue of concrete set flush to the ground. The rails told Chiun how the roof worked, and that it operated through electricity.

The roof weighed over 700 tons, so it could not be lifted, not even by the Master of Sinanju. Instead of looking at the problem as the removal of a 700-ton obstacle, Chiun considered it as a minor problem in displacing a few hundred pounds of concrete within the 700-ton obstacle in order to get a hole perhaps four feet wide.

This was a workable thing, Chiun knew, so he found a corner, because corners gave the best number of angled surfaces for striking, and chipped off a wedge with the heel of his hand. He felt the vibration of the silo roof as the concrete broke. This exposed several irregular surfaces that, when attacked, exposed more surfaces, until after several hand blows, there was a lighted hole in one corner, beneath which was a fantastic tube that glowed like a pinball machine and a Titan II missile poised in the center of the tube like a gargantuan white lipstick.

Chiun waved for the others.

Then he dropped lightly onto the nose of the Titan, set himself, and leaped across a hundred-foot drop to a work tier set in the silo wall.

"Hey! How are we supposed to follow you?" Amanda Bull hissed from above.

"Then do not follow. I will attend to this," Chiun called back loudly enough to attract the attention of an Air Force guard, who, after a moment's contemplation, recognized Chiun's kimono as nonregulation.

"Halt, sir," the guard said, his face immobile under his white helmet in an expression that was as much government issue as his uniform. Although he didn't recognize the old Oriental, he naturally assumed that anyone wandering around a SAC installation was automatically a "sir." Which was a mistake because Chiun stepped up and there was a Rubik's Cube magically in his hand.

"Watch. Twelve seconds is the current world record."

The guard watched as Chiun's long-nailed fingers blurred, and in a twinkling the multicolored cube presented solid-colored sides.

Then the cube flew past the guard's face, and before he could recover his attention, his rifle went sailing into the air and fell just a half second after his unconscious body hit the cold floor. He never saw the foot that swept out and cracked him on the line of his jaw, just hard enough to put him to sleep, not hard enough to injure him permanently.

Chiun found a stainless steel tunnel leading away from the missile and entered it, but only after he recovered his Rubik's cube and made certain it had not been damaged.

Captain Elvin Gunn, USAF, really enjoyed hs work. No one ever understood that. No one on the "outside," that is. His wife, Ellen, thought he had a dangerous job, and when he first broke the news that he had been transferred from personnel and promoted to launch control officer with a SAC missile wing, her first words were, "Oh, my God," spoken in an Irish wail. Even after he had explained that it was an excellent career move and not really dangerous at all, she still had a difficult time with it, and watched him closely for the first signs of nervous breakdown, or at least a Valium addiction, for God's sake. And she was surprised when it never happened.

It was true that Captain Elvin Gunn controlled a nine-megaton nuclear missile aimed at a precise target in Russia, and it was also true that somewhere in the Soviet Union was an SS-13 multiple warhead missile aimed at Captain Gunn's command post. But it was really a very quiet and relaxing assignment, Gunn thought, until the world went to war, and then no one would be quiet and relaxed.

For eight hours a day, five days a week, with 45 minutes for lunch and two 10-minute coffee breaks, Captain Gunn monitored the check systems that prevented an accidental launch of the missile, which could only be launched when he received a presidential order-code that matched that day's code locked in a combination safe. Then Captain Gunn would take a special key from that safe, which activated the missile-firing system.

Captain Gunn did not have as awesome a responsibility as his wife believed. Alone, he could not activate his Titan II. Twelve feet away from his control console stood an identical one with its own launch control officer. This control officer had his own combination safe and key. Only when both keys were turned simultaneously in both consoles would the giant missile roar to life. And it was not humanly possible for one person to turn two keys in locks twelve feet apart.

So most of the time, Captain Gunn sat in a cool control room with his pipe and a paperback book. Captain Gunn, who never read except at work, usually went through six books a week. Big ones.

And he liked his job. Even the periodic examinations, which he always passed with better than 98 percent marks because he always had ample study time. It was peaceful work, despite the responsibility, and Captain Gunn enjoyed the solitude. He was not allowed to talk to his co-launch control officer for more than 30 seconds per hour.

As for the danger, he had the same answer for anyone from the "outside" who asked: "Listen, I'll start to worry the minute I have to turn that key—but I won't be worrying long." Unruffled was the word for Captain Elvin Gunn.

But when the door to his control area screeched like a twisted pipe and fell forward to allow an Asian of indeterminate origin to enter, Captain Gunn was at first so surprised, he didn't know what to do.

So he dropped his smouldering pipe and copy of *The Body* as a first reaction. He yelled in pain as a second reaction.

The reason he yelled in pain was he *was* in pain, excruciating pain. It was unlike any pain he had ever felt before, as if the 90-percent water content of his body had been suddenly heated to a boil, and the little Asian was causing it simply by holding Captain Gunn's wrists together with one impossibly strong hand and exerting the pressure of a single fingernail on his inner left wrist.

"What—hooo—what do-oooh . . . you want-t-t?" asked Captain Gunn with difficulty, trying to recall what important nerve lay in his inner left wrist. He couldn't remember any nerve being there.

"This large object you guard," the Asian asked. "How does one destroy it without causing a big boom?"

"Can't—can't be done for . . . certain. Might go up anyway."

"How does one insure that the object will not explode?"

"The warhead has to be neu—neutralized. By experts." He didn't want to answer any of the Asian's questions with the truth, but the pain was just too great, and he hadn't been trained to resist pain, just psychological stress.

"How?" he was asked.

"They use a special oil mixture . . . poured into the

warhead to neutralize the explosive detonator that triggers the nuclear explosion.''

"You feel the pain easing? Good. Where can I find this oil?''

"There's a container of it in an unmarked wall locker on the top work level, next to the warhead.''

"Excellent. Now you will let my friends into this place and I will let you rest.''

"The red switch. Press it,'' said Captain Gunn, who wondered if the Asian wasn't a revenge-crazed Vietnamese. No, that couldn't be. The Vietnamese had won. Maybe he was a revenge-crazed Jap. But Captain Gunn, who drove a Japanese car, dismissed that possibility as even more remote. The Japanese had won, too.

"This is fantastic,'' Amanda Bull said as she picked her way past a number of guards and other personnel Chiun had taken out of action earlier, and led her troops into the control area. "We're actually in a SAC missile complex.''

"Thanks to me,'' Chiun reminded her.

"Yeah . . . hey, how'd you do all this?'' Amanda said in a less agreeable voice. She felt like shooting someone to reassert her control over the operation. After all, she was Preparation Group Leader, not this Chiun character.

"I did it. That is enough,'' Chiun said as he let go of Captain Gunn's aching wrists.

"What do we do now?'' Ethel Sump asked, while the others poked at control buttons and tried to read the instrument panels.

"We neutralize the warhead,'' Chiun said firmly, and disappeared to do just that before Amanda Bull could open her mouth.

After he had gone, Amanda turned to Captain Gunn and placed the muzzle of her long-barreled target pistol under his right ear and said, "Screw this neutralization shit. Fire that missile, buster. I know you can do it without arming the warhead, right?''

"Yes, but it's aimed at Russia. The Russians won't know it's not armed. We could trigger World War III."

"I don't think that would be a good idea," Ethel Sump injected helpfully.

"Hmmm. There's got to be a way," Group Leader Bull ruminated. After a moment, she had it.

"I've got it," she said. "You hit the ignition switch— I know there's got to be one somewhere here because I watched all the NASA shots on TV—and then cut it. The missile will start to go up and then crash back into the silo."

"I'm sorry, ma'am, but I can't do that," said Captain Gunn just before Amanda Bull shot him twice under his right ear. When his body slid off the console chair and fell to the floor like an oversized beanbag, Ethel Sump asked, "What did you do that for?"

"Because we didn't need him. I think I see which switches to press."

"Oh. But what about Mr. Chiun?"

"He's getting too smart. We don't need him, either."

"Oh," said Ethel Sump slowly, looking at Captain Gunn's body, which, even dead, looked handsome and reminded her of her older brother who had died in Vietnam.

Amanda kicked the corpse to one side and slid behind the console. She pressed a button. Nothing happened. She then turned some dials, which did nothing. Then she tried the FUNCTION SELECT control. Nothing.

Frustrated, she shot at the console, which caused some lights to go on, but that was all.

"Damn," Amanda said.

"Hey! Looky here. There's another panel just like that one," someone said.

Amanda went over to it, unaware that it was the mate to the first console and not a backup, and that its launch control officer was lying out in the corridor, where Chiun had taken him unawares while he had been returning from coffee break.

Amanda tried those controls, too, but to no avail.

"Bullshit," she said, and kicked the console like someone kicking a recalcitrant vending machine.

It was then that one of the finest pieces of American engineering, a computer unit with incredible tolerances and multiple failsafe backup systems designed not to allow an accidental firing of the waiting Titan missile, hummed busily.

A red panel lit up the words SILO ROOF.

"Oh, goodie. I think we've got it working," Ethel cooed.

Then another red panel illuminated the word ENABLE, and there was a distant rumbling.

The next panel said FIRE and the rumbling became a roar.

The Master of Sinanju found the container because there was only one locked cabinet on the wall of the top tier, and after snapping the padlock, there was only one container that sloshed in that cabinet, and its heaviness suggested a very dense liquid, so the Master of Sinanju assumed that it contained the oil that would neutralize the warhead.

The next step was to gain access to the warhead, which Chiun did by leaping atop it with the oil container under one arm.

There was a spout attached to the container, but no open hole in the tip of the missile like those in cars, which Chiun had seen taking refined oil in gas stations. Chiun remembered gas stations because they smelled so bad, but Remo always insisted on stopping at them whenever they went on trips. Too bad Remo wasn't here, Chiun thought. He would know what to do. All whites know machines.

Chiun tapped the missile nose with his foot, and the hollowness that came back told him that the nose was a shell covering something within, and he could break the shell without damaging what it held.

Stooping, Chiun popped a hole in the warhead shroud

with his fingernails. Then he casually peeled large patches of alloy metal back until he was standing inside the warhead, whose sides hung down like drooping sunflower petals.

Chiun was now standing on the warhead mechanism itself, which was a slim thing like an inverted ice cream cone fixed to a complicated base. As Chiun looked for a place where the container spout could go, the silo roof above him rolled back. He paid it no mind. Once he completed his work, he would lead the others away from this place with no loss of life that could anger the Emperor Smith, who was sometimes fussy about such things, and then he would be brought to the USO—or whatever the obnoxious blonde woman called it. Then, Chiun's destiny would be assured.

But before the Master of Sinanju could locate the proper place on the warhead, the missile began to rumble and shake, and then there was a roar of fire far beneath him, and then he felt the huge missile rise under his feet, and he felt himself rising with it.

CHAPTER NINE

The first thing Remo Williams noticed when he woke up was the smell.

"Cheez, Chiun," he said thickly. "Whatever crap you're cooking is burning."

The room was silent. Remo sat up in bed, and the stiffness of his limbs and the slight peeling of the burned portions of his body both told him he had been asleep not for a few hours, but for at least a full day. Then he realized the awful smell was coming from his own body.

Remo wiped a film of some greasy substance off one leg. It looked like yellowed library paste but smelled like a cheese dip whose principal ingredients included year-old fishheads, sulphur, and a smell he could not identify, but which he imagined turtle eggs smelled like after being buried for a thousand years.

Most of his body was covered with the gunk. Remo recognized it as one of Chiun's Korean remedies. God alone knew what it was made from, and Remo preferred that He keep the information to Himself. Remo showered and dressed quickly.

It was only after he had dressed that Remo found Chiun's note, which was next to his bed, rolled up and tied with a green ribbon. Remo undid the ribbon and read the scroll:

Remo, my son:
    First, I forgive you for not telling me about the

USO, whose importance to the House of Sinanju you may or may not have realized. Do not concern yourself that your ignorance almost prevented the Master of Sinanju, who has trained you even though you are only a white and often ungrateful, from solving one of the greatest mysteries of Sinanju and thus taking his rightful place in the archives as Chiun, the Great Explainer. I am on my way to remedy your oversight, so do not be concerned about this. In Sinanju, there can be no mistakes, but only detours along the path to a final goal.

By the time you read these words, Remo, my healing balm will have done its work, and I will have taken the first steps toward fulfilling my destiny. This is an important thing, as you must realize by now, and a dangerous thing, which is why I must face this thing alone. For should anything happen to me, you will become the reigning Master, even though you are white and almost cost me this great opportunity. Do not look for me, Remo. My pilgrimage may be a long one, and I will return if it is willed by my ancestors that I return. And on that day I will explain to you what you, in your ignorance, did not realize, but for which I have, in my magnanimity, forgiven you.

Know that I do not hold against you your inability to keep your elbow straight when thrusting. Viewed against all your other inadequacies, that fault is trivial.

Although the letter was in English, the signature was in Korean, and instead of putting his formal title, name, and symbolic chop at the bottom as he usually did, the Master of Sinanju had signed the note simply, "Chiun."

"Dammit, Chiun," Remo said when he was done reading. "Why couldn't you wait around one lousy day?" Remo read the letter again, and after his fourth reading he realized it was not going to tell him what he wanted to know most—namely what in blazes Chiun was talking about. Where had he gone? And what had the USO to do with anything? Remo tried to think, but his head was fuzzy. His mouth and lips were dry. He drank three glasses of water.

Then Remo called the local time number and discovered he'd been unconscious for one day. Before he could hang up, the computer voice warbled, and then it was Smith asking, "Remo. What is going on? I've been trying to reach you since yesterday."

"Smitty? How'd you do that?"

"Never mind. Are you all right?"

"Yeah. Yeah, a little stiff, I guess. But Chiun's taken off. He left some kind of dipshit note and it doesn't make any sense. He's pissed off at me and the USO for some reason."

"He probably meant UFO," Smith said dryly.

"Huh? Oh, yeah. That's right. I forgot about them."

"Remo," Smith said. "There was a serious nuclear accident a few hours ago near Oklahoma City. A Titan II missile was activated. Fortunately, it misfired and fell back into its silo. But there were casualties, and the press has found out some of it. We couldn't keep it a secret this time."

"Great. As if I don't have enough problems with Chiun off chasing flying saucers."

"Remo. This is a grave matter. The president just called me. He's concerned. But I told him you were already on the matter."

"It all ties in with those nutty FOES people, Smitty. They dragged me out into the woods to meet a flying saucer, and I got zapped."

"I know. Chiun told me. They used ultrasonics. It's not fatal, obviously. But it could be."

"That's comforting. Look, I gotta get moving. No telling what they're up to and where Chiun is."

"Are you sure you can handle this without Chiun?"

"He's my trainer, not my babysitter," Remo said and hung up before Smith could ask questions. Remo had to find Chiun.

Remo called the FOES number, but got no answer. Now what? That had been his only lead. He could investigate the missile site that had been wasted, except that Smith hadn't told him which site it was, and Remo didn't feel like calling old lemon puss back right now. Never mind hassling with military idiots at the site who would probably shoot at him and inconvenience him in other minor ways.

That left the spot where Remo had been zapped by the whatever-it-was with the lights. Might as well try that, he thought and left, not bothering to close or to lock the door behind him. He wondered if he still smelled of Chiun's ointment. . . .

The Master of Sinanju was keeping his temper under control. It was not easy. Had he not gotten the blonde woman and her friends into the missile place? Had he not told the blonde woman that he was going to neutralize the missile, which was what she had wanted? Had he not then left her sight only a few minutes? Had he not also done all of her work for her despite her ineptitude—and nearly completed the task, when he found the missile on which he stood rising from its hole when it was not necessary?

Yes, he had. He had put up with her stupidity, her ignorance, and her lack of proper respect toward the Master of Sinanju.

And what had his reward been?

His reward was to find himself atop a missile that was going to land in the barbarian land of the Russias.

It was fortunate, the Master of Sinanju told himself, that an object of that size and weight did not rise rapidly in the beginning, that its initial movement was vibration, which the Master could detect, and that when the fire began streaming from its tail, the missile lifted slowly against gravity at first. Very slowly.

Chiun had waited until the warhead came level with the open roof before he stepped off it onto the ground outside, where two great horns of fire were shooting up at opposite angles. These were exhaust flames carried up by deflector vents, although Chiun did not know this. He only knew they were dangerous and so avoided them. He also knew that once the missile escaped its hole, it would spill even more flame behind it, and because he did not know how much flame, he jumped from its path. And the missile rose in thunder, like a tree growing out of the earth faster than trees could grow, but still slowly compared to the speed of Sinanju.

Chiun had made it to the shelter of the control bunker when the missile fell back into its hole and exploded. It was not so much an explosion as it was a falling and bursting apart. But there had been no mushroom cloud, so Chiun knew he was in no danger. He also knew that if there had been a mushroom cloud, he would not have seen it anyway, and there would now be a new Master of Sinanju, and the old Master—himself—would have been cheated of his rightful destiny.

"I'm sorry," Amanda Bull was saying as the FOES van tore off into the night, leaving behind a ruined Titan II missile, one of the most destructive devices known to man.

"You have caused destruction and death where none was necessary," Chiun told her as he arranged his robes so the seat would not wrinkle them.

"It was an accident," Group Leader Amanda Bull lied. "I pressed the button by accident."

"And did you kill that man by accident, too?"

"How did you know about him?"

"There is blood on your clothes and a smell on your weapon that tells me it has been fired. Who else would you kill?"

"It was necessary. Besides, we should all count ourselves lucky that I found the abort button in time. It could've been a lot worse."

Chiun sniffed audibly. "Emperor Smith will be displeased. My village depends upon his gold."

"I don't know what you're talking about," Amanda said. "I already said I was sorry."

"I'm sorry, too, Mr. Chiun," Ethel Sump said.

"I accept your apology, but not hers," Chiun told Ethel. Then he asked, "Where are we going?"

"We have to report our glorious victory," Amanda said.

"We are going to meet the USO?" Chiun asked hopefully, leaning forward.

"That's right. And you're coming, too."

Chiun sat back in his seat, and his face assumed a benevolent smile. "You shall be rewarded for your efforts," he told Amanda.

"Just why do you want to meet our leader?" she asked.

Chiun's smile evaporated. He looked out the window at the black trees flashing past.

"Because his ancestors knew my ancestors," Chiun said finally.

The ship was not waiting at the rendezvous when they arrived. Amanda cut the engine and beeped the horn three times. Everyone got out of the van and turned his eyes skyward, but there was nothing but stars and ragged clouds up there.

When the white fire burst into life over their heads a few minutes later, the Oklahoma City chapter of the Flying Object Evaluation Center sent up a collective "OOOOoooohhhh!"

Chiun alone was silent, his hazel eyes fixed sharply on the descending spaceship.

The UFO sprouted red and green secondary lights and passed over their heads after proving it could remain stationary in the air. It floated over the trees and sank. A misty, milky glow showed through the forest wall.

"Okay, everybody," Amanda Bull said proudly. "Let's report."

They marched toward the light, Amanda Bull leading the way, Chiun behind her and carrying himself like a bride walking down the aisle, with the other FOES members strung out behind them.

"This is a great day," Chiun said in a solemn voice.

"It sure is," Ethel Sump giggled.

When they were gathered before the shining object, Chiun whispered to Amanda, "You must properly introduce me, woman."

"Yeah, yeah. Let me report first, will you?" Amanda strode forward and disappeared through the ship's door, which opened for her, then closed. The lights dimmed so they didn't hurt the eyes so much.

Not long after, Amanda returned and told Chiun, "The World Master will see you now."

Chiun took a step backward, disgust on his wrinkled face. "I have not been properly introduced. You must present me as Chiun, the reigning Master of Sinanju."

"Come on, come on. We haven't got all night."

"Ingrate."

And so Chiun, lifting the hem of his kimono to keep it out of the tall grass, stepped up to the shining object and with measured tread, passed within. He found himself in a semicircular room like the inside of a steel ball that had been partitioned off. On the face of the partition was a pebbled-glass screen and beyond that, a wavering shadow.

Chiun stepped up to the glass and bowed once. "I am Chiun, reigning Master of Sinanju, latest in the line of Masters of Sinanju, who traces his ancestry back to the Master Wang the Greater, and even before him."

"Yes, I know, Chiun, Master of Sinanju. For I am a Master too. I am the World Master, who is known as Hopak Kay."

A strange expression crossed Chiun's face, and then he said, "We have much to discuss, you and I. May I enter your chambers?"

"No. It is forbidden. Nor may I leave my chambers, for I must breathe, which I cannot do in your atmosphere."

"Ah," said Chiun. "I understand. Breathing is important to us, too."

"Preparation Group Leader Bull has informed me you wish to join with our movement to bring peace to the world."

"A worthy goal, World Master," Chiun replied. "And it demonstrates your wisdom, and the wisdom of your house, that you have chosen to bring your civilizing influence to this land above all others, for it sorely needs it. America is a land of ugliness, although one time in its past it produced many beautiful dramas, although even these have slipped into decadence."

"Yes," World Master Hopak Kay said reedily, "when I am ready to announce myself to the world, we will usher in a new era in which drama will be raised to new heights of artistry. All will be allowed to express themselves in the manner of their choosing."

"Except those who are inferior. There are many who are inferior in this world. There are the whites and then the blacks, and after them the Chinese and Japanese . . .''

"Yes," the World Master agreed, "all inferior peoples must be dealt with accordingly."

"Of course," added Chiun, who had been told by Remo that racial discrimination was a bad thing, "all inferior races must be tolerated and treated as if they are equal, even when we know they are not."

"Yes, all inferior races must be dealt with as if they were not inferior. You are very wise."

Chiun nodded his head happily. Here was an obviously superior being, he thought. Here was someone who thought logically and saw truth clearly. "The House of

Sinanju acknowledges your wisdom as well. May I ask the name of your house?''

The shadow moved briefly behind the glass, and for a strange second, the Master of Sinanju thought he perceived that the World Master had two arms on the left side of his body, but of course that was impossible. . . .

"House?" the voice asked, puzzled.

"Yes, what is the name of the place from whence you come, the place of your ancestors?''

"I am from the House of Betelgeuse."

Chiun bowed again. "It is good that the House of Sinanju again meets the House of Beetle Goose. Long has the House of . . ."

"Alert! Alert!" Amanda Bull screeched from outside. "That Remo is back! He's back!"

Chiun's head whipped around. "Remo, my son."

Then from outside there came the flat cracks of shots and noises of confusion and panic.

Remo Williams was in the middle of the local FOES chapter, where he had moved after dodging the first few bullets aimed at him. Despite some lingering stiffness resulting from his earlier brush with the UFO, he still moved easily. He had been surprised to find everyone back in the same location, but that hadn't slowed his reflexes any.

In the middle of the milling group, where they didn't dare shoot for fear of hitting one another, Remo began taking them out one at a time. There was a fat guy in overalls to his right, and Remo dropped him with a straight-fingered jab to the base of the neck, interrupting the signals from brain to limbs with a slight dislocation of the upper vertebrae.

Next, Remo side-kicked a kneecap, and someone else dropped, yelling with pain.

The third person went down with two bullets in her lungs, which Amanda Bull put there because she obviously didn't care about hurting her own people to get at Remo.

So Remo floated to the left and started to come up on her blind side, where the raised rifle butt cut off her peripheral vision.

"Remo, stop that. Stop that this instant. What are you doing?" It was Chiun's voice, high and squeaky. He had come from somewhere and was standing in front of the dingbat UFO, Remo saw, his hands upraised and the sleeves of his kimono hanging off to expose his frail arms. He was all but jumping up and down.

"Chiun," Remo yelled back. "Get clear. That big thing's what burned me!"

"Remo. Stop this instant."

"*Preparation Group Leader*," the amplified voice of the World Master announced, "*we must evacuate. Bring your people.*"

Amanda Bull instantly dropped back, shouting, "Everybody into the ship!" She evaded Remo only because Remo had been brought up short by Chiun's yelling, and he wasn't sure what was going on.

He was even more confused when the group piled into the UFO, including the wounded, who had to be helped. Chiun was one of the helpers.

"Chiun, what the ding-dong hell are you up to?" Remo called out to him, not wanting to venture too close to the UFO.

"Okay, we're going up," Amanda Bull shouted as the UFO slowly lifted like a soap bubble from a child's plastic loop. It did not hum, so Remo didn't run. He didn't come any closer, either.

"I am coming, too," Chiun said, but even as he did, the opening in the UFO hull shut on him.

"Wait," Chiun cried out forlornly. "Take me with you. I am the Master of Sinanju, and you must not forget me."

But the ship, a brilliant ball of light, sailed off into the darkness, leaving Chiun with a stricken expression on his face and a bewildered Remo beside him in the empty clearing.

"Chiun, what the hell is going on?" Remo asked. "I got your note."

Slowly, the Master of Sinanju turned to face his pupil, his clear eyes ablaze with a light that sent a sick feeling into the pit of Remo's stomach. For a full minute, Chiun said nothing, but finally he puffed out his cheeks in rage and said in a quavering voice, "You are no longer my son, Remo Williams. Do not ever address me again."

CHAPTER TEN

The first thing Pavel Zarnitsa did upon arriving in Oklahoma City was check the Yellow Pages for Mexican restaurants, and he found, to his horror, that there were none.

"Sukin Syn," he said in anguish, loud enough for a passing TWA pilot to overhear. The pilot, carrying his flight instructions under his arm, stopped at the open phone booth and asked engagingly if Pavel was by chance from the Soviet Union.

"No," Pavel told him curtly, not turning around. "I am not."

"No?" the pilot asked, puzzled. "I picked up some Russian on overseas runs. I could have sworn I heard you say 'son of a bitch' in Russian."

"I did not. Go away please."

"No need to be rude, sir," said the pilot, who liked to make a good impression on foreign visitors. "You're obviously not from this country, and I was just being friendly. Just what kind of accent is that, by the way?"

"I haff not the accent," Pavel told him in thick English. Not being in America to spy on Americans, he had never gone through speech modification sessions. He was supposed to sound Russian.

"Sure you do," said the other, who was now becoming suspicious. "Where are you from, if you don't mind my asking?"

"I do mind," said the KGB man, pretending to riffle through the Yellow Pages.

"Need help looking up something? I see you're having trouble there."

"Why, yes . . . I am looking for a place which sells tacos."

"Tacos? Hmmm. About the only place hereabouts carrying those things is that Irish bar on West Street. Name escapes me, but it's easy to find."

Pavel Zarnitsa abruptly turned around with a false grin on his face. "To you, I am grateful. Good-bye," he said as he brushed by.

The cab driver also asked about his accent, and Pavel briefly considered taking the pieces of the plastic pistol from his suitcase and assembling them. The pistol was spring-driven, like a zip gun, and it would easily go through the car seat and into the driver's back. It would not do to call attention to himself in any way, but Pavel decided a dead body was worse than a puzzled driver, so he changed his mind.

"I know," the driver bellowed as they pulled up before the Will Rogers Lucky Shamrock Bar and Grill. "You're a Polack!"

"A what?"

"You know—one of those guys from Poland. We get a lot of you people since the Russkies busted up the union."

"Yes, that is right," Pavel told him as he paid the fare. "I am Polack. Good-bye to you."

Pavel Zarnitsa walked up to the bar, happy he had not killed the cab driver. Now he had a reasonable explanation for his awkward accent.

"A Scootch and three tacos, please," he told the bartender.

"A *what* and three tacos?"

"Scootch. On the rocks."

"I getcha. Scotch on the rocks," he said, setting the drink before the black-haired customer.

"Please do not mind my accent," Pavel told him. "I am a Polack, new to your country."

"That so?" the bartender said as he took three frozen packets from an under-counter freezer, stripped them, and put them in a sizzling Fry-o-lator, where they immediately turned the color of dry soil. "Most Polish people don't like being called Polacks. Nice to meet someone different."

"I am a very reasonable Polack," Pavel said, sipping his Scotch. "I even like Russians. Are you not going to make my tacos?"

"That's them in the Fry-o-lator."

"Really? I have never seen them prepared before. I did not know they were fried in oil. Amazing. How long do they take?"

"Done now," the bartender said, dumping the tacos onto a plate next to Pavel's Scotch.

Pavel took an eager bite and didn't know whether to chew or spit. He chewed slowly and swallowed with difficulty. A ghastly expression settled on his strongly molded features. Doubtfully, he forced himself to eat the whole thing.

"I do not understand," he said finally. "This taco is hard. The shell is hard, not soft as in New York. And I tasted no meat."

"This ain't New York buddy. I don't make 'em on the premises. They come in frozen and I unfreeze 'em. No meat, either. Just refried bean filling."

"Pah! These are not tacos. These are fakes!"

"I can get you something else . . ."

"You can get me another Scootch," Pavel said miserably. "I am no longer hungry."

"Suit yourself."

After fortifying himself with another drink, Pavel gave thought to his investigation into the strange newspaper reports suggesting something was wrong with America's missile bases. It would not do to personally approach any

United States installation, even without the problem of his accent. How then? . . . Of course, he thought. The bartender. All bartenders the world over are repositories of information picked up from their customers.

"I have been reading in the papers about the strange things that have been happening in this area," Pavel said casually.

"Strange? Oh, you mean the flying saucers some folks have been seeing. Yeah, I had a guy in here two nights ago who claimed he saw one down near Chickasha. Said it was big and bright and sailed right over his car without making a sound. Can you beat that? Myself, I don't believe anything I don't see with my own eyes, but I gotta admit this guy sure *thought* he saw something."

"Really?" Pavel searched his memory. He had heard of the term flying saucers, better known as Unidentified Flying Objects. They had them in Russia, too. In fact, he had once come across a reference to a KGB file on UFOs, but it was classified. He had wondered why the Committee would have such a file.

"Where would I find more information on these flying saucers?" Pavel demanded.

"There's a bunch that's got an office a couple of blocks up. In the Stigman Building. Call themselves FOES, and are supposed to know everything there is to know about them things. Had one as a customer once, but all he did was babble about some kind of government conspiracy."

No one answered when Pavel Zarnitsa knocked on the door of the FOES office, and even though he knew there might not be a direct connection between the sighting of flying saucers in Oklahoma and the strangeness within the Strategic Air Command, the two occurrences could be linked, so he forced the door.

Both the reception area and office were empty. In a drawer of the office desk, he found a map of Oklahoma on which every SAC missile installation was clearly marked, along with notes on approach routes. There were other

materials—newspaper clippings on nuclear missiles, a list
of FOES chapters across the country and their members.
There was also a list of names headed ''Preparation Group
Two,'' which began with someone known as Preparation
Group Leader Amanda Bull.

Checking the office Rolodex, Pavel found addresses and
telephone numbers for everyone on that list.

''Incredible,'' he said to himself, sinking into a chair.
''These lunatic Americans are trying to destroy their own
country's missiles.''

Pavel began calling each of the numbers. There was no
answer on the first two, and when he called the third, he
got a frantic woman who at first thought it was her husband calling. She hadn't seen him in two days, when he
abruptly left for ''one of his ridiculous flying saucer out-
ings,'' as she put it. It turned out several others had done
the same thing. Still others didn't answer their phones.

He dialed another number.

''Ethel Sump speaking.''

''You fool!'' a woman's sharp voice called from the
background somewhere. ''We're not supposed to be here.
Hang up!''

''Oh, I forgot,'' Ethel said, and hung up.

That was enough for Pavel Zarnitsa. For some reason,
these people were involved in the missile incident, and
they were hiding out at the home of a woman named Ethel
Sump, whose address card went into his wallet, as Pavel
went out the door.

Amanda Bull was livid.

''These people are idiots,'' she fumed, as she paced back
and forth while waiting for the shadowy image of the
World Master to show itself against the pebbled glass.
She couldn't understand how Ethel Sump could be so stupid as to pick up the phone. Who knew who could have
been on the other line. Since their triumph the other
night, secrecy had become crucial. The military was cer-

tainly out there investigating the destruction of their missile. And that Remo whatshisface already knew too much. But there was no time to find and liquidate him. There hadn't been enough time to sneak back to the office and remove any of the Preparation Group plans, either. *Anyone* could find those. That was why, after the incident with Remo, it had become necessary to hide out with Ethel Sump, who had inherited a decrepit farmhouse. It was the only place big enough and remote enough for them all.

But two days of inactivity had begun to wear on everyone's nerves. Something had to be done.

The shadow showed eerily against the glass in response to Amanda's knock. Amanda stopped pacing.

"Yes, Preparation Group Leader. You have something to report?"

"That stupid Ethel answered the phone when it rang— against my explicit instructions. Discipline is becoming a big problem."

"Who was calling?" the World Master inquired reedily.

"I don't know. She hung up before they said anything."

"That was unwise. It may have aroused suspicion where none existed."

"Should I punish her?" Amanda asked. "I feel like punishing someone. I haven't felt this much like punishing anyone since my husband left me."

"No. There are more important matters before us. I have not yet finished repairing the damage to my craft. It must remain concealed in this barn for at least another day."

"Damn!" Amanda said. "We're all sitting ducks if we're discovered here." She began to pace again, her boots clicking on metal flooring. She pulled at her hair. "Is there anything I can do to help? There must be! Two hands are better than one. If we can get this ship going again, we can all escape to—"

"No, Amanda Bull. I overestimated the ability of my

craft to carry human beings through your atmosphere. The strain of bearing Preparation Group Two to this place taxed my propulsion unit. It can be repaired in time. But I must never again attempt such a thing.''

A dark notch of perplexity showed between Amanda's eyes.

''I don't get it,'' she said. ''How could the weight of twelve people damage a spaceship that carried you all the way across the universe?''

''Because, Preparation Group Leader Bull, my ship is designed to travel in space, where the forces of gravity are not in operation. In your atmosphere, under Earth's gravity, my ship moves less efficiently. Further, you humans weigh more than my people. I miscalculated that factor, resulting in the temporary crippling of the gravitation spheres I have told you about. Do you understand this explanation?''

Amanda nodded her head thoughtfully. ''I think so. Yes . . . it makes sense now. Sure.''

''Good. You will repeat my explanation to the others so that their minds are eased. In the meantime, there is work to be done.''

''What kind? I'm ready.''

''Our second attempt to destroy an American missile was a success. But it has also alerted those who guard those missiles. Our task is now more difficult, and we must compensate for our success.''

''Compensate for our success? . . .''

''Yes,'' the World Master said slowly, bringing both sets of pipestem arms to the level of his big head. Amanda felt a chill ripple along her back. ''It will be difficult to destroy so many dangerous missiles ourselves. Preparation Group One is no more. We are unable to recruit a third preparation group at this time. But our numbers are sufficient to influence the many nuclear disarmament groups. Influence them, and they will influence the United States government to dismantle all nuclear weapons.''

"Do you think we can do that?"

"Yes. We need only demonstrate the danger of such weapons."

"Ho-ow do we do that?" Amanda asked as a sickness settled deep in her stomach.

"The warhead of the missile you so courageously destroyed is still intact. They will attempt to move it from its silo and dispose of it secretly. Station someone in the area. When the warhead is moved, you will capture it and bring it here. I will decide what will be done with it at that time."

"You—you're not going to explode the warhead, are you?"

"I will decide that when you have successfully completed your task."

"But . . ."

"Do not question my instructions, nor the glorious destiny in which you share. I am your brain, Amanda Bull. Remember that. I am your brain. You are dismissed."

The figure of the World Master receded behind the concealing glass and grew indistinct.

Amanda swallowed hard. The sick feeling in her stomach felt more like a hot catching of her breath. It was that feeling again. Only this time there was no sense of exhilaration. There was just the fear.

She left the ship, which stood in the cool confines of a barn. None of the craft's lights were on, but it floated three feet above the ground. When they had first pushed the weakened object into the barn, it had floated all the way to the top. The antigravity generators—or whatever they were—had been sluggish all during the flight to the Sump farm. Once Amanda ordered everyone off, the ship began to rise uncontrollably. It had been all they could do to get it into the barn and shut the doors. It had been Martin Cannell who suggested they throw a big net over the ship and stake it down. That had worked.

Checking the stakes again, Amanda saw that they were

unaffected by the pull of the levitating spacecraft. Probably they would hold until the World Master had everything going again. That was good, Amanda thought. She didn't need more problems at a time like this.

"Oooh, here she comes!" Ethel Sump breathed; watching Amanda Bull approach the farmhouse, where nothing had grown since her parents had left it to her.

"I hope she has good news," Martin Cannell said. "I'm getting tired of waiting around."

"Shut up, all of you!" Amanda barked when the others crowded around her like eager children. "We've got new orders."

"What are they?" one woman named Marsha asked warily.

"We're going to steal what's left of the nuclear warhead we wrecked," Amanda said sternly.

There was a long moment of breathless silence in the farmhouse.

"Isn't that kinda . . . risky, Amanda?" Ethel asked.

"It's got to be done. And we've got to move fast. The Air Force could move the warhead to another location at any time. I want half of you to come with me, and the other half will stay here until I call. Volunteers step forward!"

There was another uncomfortable silence.

"I said, volunteers step forward, damn it!"

But no one stepped forward.

"All right, what's wrong?" Amanda demanded of the fidgeting group.

"Ummm. Some of us feel bad about the people who got killed last time," Ethel Sump said slowly.

Amanda frowned. "I feel bad, too."

"Yeah, but you did some of the killing yourself," someone muttered. "And you got one of us by accident."

"That's right," Ethel said. "And you shot that nice officer. He didn't do anything. And he was handsome, too."

"I had no choice, you know. Our glorious work must go on. Or have you all forgotten what this is all about? We're trying to save the world from itself. If a few people have to die, that's a small price to pay to keep all the military idiots from blowing the whole freaking world up."

The others looked at one another sheepishly. No one looked directly at their blonde leader.

"Now I need six people," Amanda said, placing a hand on the automatic clipped to her Sam Browne belt.

"Okay, I'll go," Ethel said. "But no more killing."

"Me, too."

"Count me in."

"Good," Amanda said, relieved that a full-scale mutiny had been avoided and she wouldn't have to shoot anyone as an example. Shooting people didn't seem to solve problems as much as she expected it would. Sometimes it even made things worse.

Giving that realization more thought, she ordered the group to load weapons and equipment into the FOES van.

Thad Screiber had chased Unidentified Flying Objects across 47 of the 50 states in his time and had never experienced a close encounter of *any* kind. Yet he had grossed $25,000 last year alone.

Thad was a writer, and a specialist in UFOs. He had never seen one, didn't care to ever see one, and if the truth were ever to be known, he did not even believe in them. But he made his living interviewing people who said they saw flying saucers, so he took the subject seriously when he was in the field.

The field this time was Oklahoma, where a flurry of wire service copy about motorists sighting strange objects in the sky brought him running. But in two days he had not been able to locate any one of these people. That was bad. Without interviews, he couldn't write articles for any of the various magazines that published his work under his various pen names. It didn't matter who he interviewed, so long as that person could be quoted as having seen something. Thad Screiber was not paid to judge the reliability of those he interviewed.

Instead, frustrated, he drove his Firebird along the highways south of Oklahoma City. He had just decided to return home when he pulled into a roadside gas station.

"Ten bucks, regular," Thad instructed the attendant, and turned on his pocket tape recorder just in case. "Lot of people claiming to see some strange sights around this area, I hear," Thad remarked casually.

"Could be," the attendant said absently, running the hose to the car. "But I ain't one of 'em."

"No? To hear some people tell it, the air is thick with flying saucers here."

"Well, about the only funny thing I've seen lately was one of those jazzed-up vans come barreling down the road not twenty minutes back. Come to think of it, it had flyin' saucers and such stuff painted on the sides."

"That so?" asked Thad, who decided that "Mystery Van Linked to Oklahoma UFO Sightings" might make an article. "Could you describe it?"

"Well . . . it was brown, had one of them bubble tops, lots of doodads and the like. Goin' pretty darn fast, too."

"That's interesting," Thad said as he tendered a $10 bill. "What's your name?"

"Bill."

"Okay, Bill. Thanks a lot."

Thad drove off, dictating into the recorder: "While no one knows the true motives of the mystery van, a gas company official who fearfully declined to give his full name, described the vehicle as brown and covered with cryptic designs. More importantly, his description mysteriously *lacked any references to wheels or the driver* of this 'van,' which he claimed, in awestruck tones, was *traveling unusually fast*. Was this phantom really an earthly van, or could it have been a drone scouting craft disguised to resemble . . ."

A roadblock interrupted his narrative. Thad had only to see the sawhorses and military vehicles and uniforms down the road before he hung a U-turn and went back the way he came. A detour brought him west of the roadblock, where trees were thick.

Something tall and metallic glittered beyond those trees and, his curiosity aroused, Thad pulled over, dug out his high-powered binoculars, and clambered to the roof of his car.

What he saw through those binoculars made him forget about Unidentified Flying Objects.

Thad Screiber saw the sun reflecting off a giant crane, which held up what was left of a Titan II missile, while a team of men attempted to maneuver the burnt weapon into one end of a giant canister. The canister was part of an eight-wheeled truck, and Thad recognized it as the kind of truck they used to ferry rockets to launching pads for NASA. Except that this missile was being secretly handled in an Oklahoma wheat field and was shattered beyond repair. Whatever had happened here, Thad knew, the world should know about.

CHAPTER ELEVEN

"It's awful big," Martin Cannell said for the seventh or eighth time.

"It's bigger than big," Ethel Sump breathed. "It's *humongous*!"

"Shut up, both of you! I'm thinking."

"Well, I hope you can think of a way to steal that missile without anyone being killed," Martin said ruefully. "Especially us. The tires on that missile-carrying thing are about as big as our whole van, Amanda."

For hours, they had watched the missile-loading operation from a safe distance. They had known something was happening at the SAC base when they were turned away from a military roadblock, so they turned back, stashed the van in a clump of foliage, and infiltrated the cordoned-off area on foot. It had not been difficult because the government had simply blocked all approach routes to the base to discourage traffic. They hadn't expected foot traffic in such a sparsely populated area.

Amanda had felt good about that, but now she was nervous, contemplating the task of commandeering something the size of a missile-carrier. But now, with the missile loaded and the carrier getting ready to trundle its cargo onto the highway, she was at a total loss for an idea that might work. The truck's diesel engine sounded like faraway thunder.

"Look! It's leaving," Ethel said.

Laboriously, the carrier got underway, its massive tires

gouging and chewing the soft earth. A smaller truck followed in its wake, and was in turn tailed by an unobtrusive stepvan. The three vehicles joined up with a number of others on the main road and formed a slow column.

"Wait a minute!" Martin said, grabbing Amanda's field glasses. "Let me—Hah! I was right. Look—on the side of the thing like a delivery truck."

Amanda looked. "So? It's some symbol or some—"

"That's the symbol for nuclear stuff. You see them on fallout shelters all the time."

"So what?" Amanda snapped, pulling at her nose.

"I'll bet the warhead is in that small truck! Sure, they wouldn't load the whole missile if the warhead was still attached. It would be too dangerous."

"I think Martin is right, Amanda," Ethel said loudly. She was beginning to like Martin. And he was single.

"Quiet," said Amanda, who didn't like the idea of Martin being right about something for the second time in two days. "Even if that's true, we're still going to have to take on that whole group of trucks and soldiers."

But a moment later, they all saw the moving column divide, with the small truck that presumably bore the warhead taking another fork.

"This is our chance, everyone!" Amanda shouted. "Back to the van. We're going to head that truck off."

Even at a dead run, it took a while to return to the waiting van, which was outside the military cordon. Then they had to figure out where the truck was going in order to intercept it.

"Go south, and take the second exit," Martin told Amanda. "That should take us exactly where we want to be. You know, I'll bet they deliberately sent the warhead off in another direction. You know, that missile truck is so big, it's bound to attract attention. But who's going to notice a dinky little truck?"

Amanda pushed the accelerator to 80. "Maybe," she said.

There was no sign of the truck in question when they reached the road where they expected it to show up. Amanda stopped, and swerved the van so it blocked the road.

"Okay," she said. "Weapons at the ready. We'll just wait for it."

"I've a better idea," Martin said.

"I don't want to hear it," Amanda growled.

"But what's to stop the truck from backing up and going the other way when they see us?"

That made sense even to Amanda, who was doing a slow burn. Why were men such egotists, she asked herself. Always showing off and grabbing at the credit for everything.

"We'll split up and hide on either side of the road," Amanda said quickly, before anyone could make another suggestion, "then jump out and surround them when they stop."

"I was going to suggest that," Martin said.

"I'll bet you were," Amanda said sarcastically. "C'mon, let's get to it."

They got to it, and before long the stepvan with the black-circle-and-three-yellow-triangle symbol for nuclear energy rolled into sight. It stopped close to the gaudy FOES van, and the driver honked his horn twice sharply.

When half a dozen armed commandos jumped out of the trees, he stopped honking and threw the gears into reverse. A bullet knocked the passenger window all over the cab, and he ceased that effort, too. He threw up his hands as the black-clad group surrounded him.

"I'm unarmed," he called out, which was true. He noticed that most of his assailants were women, and at least two of them were on the chunky side. *What the hell's going on*? he thought, as he touched a floor button with his toe, causing a light to go on in the back of the truck, where it would alert a radiation-suited guard.

"Out of the truck," Amanda ordered.

The driver got out, and as he turned his back on her, Amanda clubbed him unconscious with a rifle butt.

"See? No killing," Amanda said to all concerned, as they dragged the driver off to the roadside, where he would later be run over by a drunken motorist.

That done, they tried to open the back of the truck. It was padlocked. Standing off to one side, Amanda fired three shots at the lock, two of which caused it to snap open.

When they opened up the back, they found a scarred and blackened nuclear warhead. They also found a guard whose white plastic radiation garments were streaked with his own blood. He gurgled once, dropped his rifle, and then dropped dead.

"Gee, Amanda," Ethel said, small-voiced. "You must have got him by accident."

"I couldn't help it," Amanda complained. "They should buy them bullet-proof vests or something. Anyway, we've got the warhead. Let's get out of here."

They shut up the truck. Amanda took the wheel. Ethel and the others returned to the van, and the two vehicles rapidly left the area.

At first, Thad Screiber was going to give his story to one of the wire services because they paid more than a newspaper would. But years of writing articles for *Destiny* magazine and *Flying Saucer Factual* had earned him plenty of money and little glory. So Thad decided to go for the glory and called the editor of the *New York Times* from the first pay phone he came across. After haggling for a minute, they struck an agreement, and Thad began dictating his eyewitness account of the salvage of a destroyed American nuclear missile, which would carry his actual byline—something that had not happened since his first reporting job on a hometown weekly.

It was a good feeling, Thad reflected, as he returned to his car. Perhaps this was what writing was really all about.

You write what you believe in and are proud enough to sign your right name to it. Maybe it was time to retire all those phony pen names and go back to real reporting.

Then, just as he started his car, a brown van with a bubble roof and emblazoned with scenes right out of Thad's own articles sped past. It was followed by a stepvan plainly—but disturbingly—marked with the nuclear symbol.

Some long-dormant reporter's sixth sense told him that he should follow them both. It was only a hunch, but something about what he'd seen made him wonder if there might not be a connection between UFO activity in Oklahoma and the mysterious nuclear accident that had incapacitated a Titan missile.

Thad fell in behind the two trucks.

CHAPTER TWELVE

It has been the worst two days of Remo Williams's life.

Chiun had been mad at him before. Someone who didn't know the old Korean well could easily get the impression that Chiun was *always* mad at Remo, but that wasn't so. Chiun scolded Remo because that was Chiun's responsibility as Remo's teacher. To err might be human, but to err in Sinanju was to die. Chiun knew this and Remo knew this. And there had been a time or two when Remo had seriously offended Chiun. At those times, Chiun became a stranger, and Remo knew that his relationship with the man who was both father and teacher to him was in jeopardy. Usually, Remo's serious offenses were offenses against Sinanju and its traditions and not against Chiun himself. Not even Remo's close relationship with Chiun protected him there. But Remo, who respected Chiun and now belonged to Sinanju, never knowingly insulted Sinanju traditions and was always forgiven for what Chiun called his "unfortunate ignorance."

But this time it was different. Seriously different.

From the time the UFO had taken everyone except Chiun away, the Master of Sinanju had refused to speak to Remo. Remo had tried to convince Chiun to return to their hotel with him. Chiun had not refused. He had simply walked off. No abuse and no arguments. He just started walking in the general direction of Oklahoma City.

Remo had followed him.

"Don't tell me you intend to walk all the way back,

Chiun," he said. "It's gotta be at least thirty miles. C'mon back to the car."

Chiun walked along in stiff silence.

"Look, if you want to be mad for some reason, you can be just as mad riding in the back seat as walking."

A breeze stirred Chiun's sparse hair as he walked.

"Then at least you can tell me what you're mad about."

No answer.

"Look, Chiun. I think you owe me an explanation at least," Remo said, touching Chiun's arm.

No swirl of robes betrayed Chiun's intent, but the Master of Sinanju spun fully around without breaking stride, his right arm slashed once, and he continued on.

"Begone, vile one," Chiun called back.

Remo looked down at his chest where Chiun's deadly fingernail had laid open his T-shirt and created a thin pressure mark across his chest. A quarter-inch more and Remo would be leaking blood.

In shocked silence, Remo returned to his car alone.

It had been no better when, hours later, Chiun found his way back. Remo looked up as Chiun entered the hotel room, but the old man ignored him and walked to the telephone.

"I wish to speak to someone in charge. Good. I have a complaint. There is someone in my room who does not belong. You will send someone to remove him? Thank you."

"This has gone far enough, Little Father," Remo had said.

"I am no one's father," Chiun retorted. He opened the door to the hall and waited.

When the manager arrived, looking harried, Chiun leveled a trembling arm at Remo and cried, "I found this stranger in my room, and now he refuses to leave. I demand his removal."

"Little Father . . ." Remo began, angrily.

"See? He is claiming that I am his father. Anyone can see this is not so," Chiun shouted loudly enough to carry into the hall. A crowd collected at the door.

"Well?" the manager asked Remo.

"Aw, he's just ticked at me for some reason."

"Are you this man's son?" the manager asked levelly. The crowd muttered their skepticism.

"I'm registered in this room," Remo said. "You can check it out. Remo Williams."

"He lies!" Chiun crowed. "He told me his name was Remo Greeley. This is proof of his deception."

"This room *is* registered to a Remo Greeley," the manager pointed out.

"Okay, okay," Remo said, throwing up his hands. "I'm leaving. This old coot is right. He's not my father. I don't have a father. And what's more, I never *had* a father."

Remo pushed past the crowd, who roundly jeered at him. He registered in another hotel, angrier with Chiun than he'd ever been before. He didn't sleep that night, but by morning his anger had drained. He called Chiun's number, but when he said, "It's me," Chiun hung up without a word. It was not Chiun's way to be so brittle, and Remo felt a growing fear. Perhaps this time he had done something so unforgivable that Chiun really had disowned him. But what? And what did UFOs have to do with it?

Remo wondered if Smith might know, and called him. But Smith was frantic.

"Remo, my God! What have you done? Chiun told me he is resigning as your trainer. I couldn't talk him out of it."

"Yeah, yeah, I know all that. But did he tell you what's pissed him off?"

"No, he refused to discuss it." Pause. "You mean you don't know yourself?" Smith asked incredulously. "How could you be so irresponsible? How could—"

Remo had hung up on Smith, angry again. For two days he had felt angry and scared and even lost by turns. He felt like an orphan again. He didn't know what to do. He had never been without Chiun for any length of time and was surprised at how much he had grown to depend upon the old Korean in small ways. What would happen to him now? Would he continue to develop along the path of Sinanju, or would he be frozen at this stage of development? And what about Chiun? Would he return to Korea?

There were too many questions, and Remo had thought of them all. By the end of the second day, he still had no answers. The FOES office had been empty when he checked it the day before, but Remo decided to try again. If he could grab just one of those nuts, he might have something. And he was still on an assignment, even if he didn't feel like completing it.

A car pulled up alongside Remo as he walked down the street. It was growing dark now, and he was in a bad section of the city. Remo knew this because the one police car he had seen went through the area rapidly, its two officers staring straight ahead as if they didn't want to see anything that might require their attention.

"Can you help me out, fella?" the driver called out to Remo.

"You lost?" Remo asked, leaning on the car.

"No," the driver said. He slid across to the passenger's window, showing the stubby nose of a Saturday night special. "I just need money. Yours."

"Nice gun," Remo said conversationally. "How come you need money? Don't you work?"

"This is my work. Hand over your wallet, or I'll blow your freaking brains out."

"I think you should find a new line of work," Remo said.

"Yeah?"

"Yeah," Remo said, bringing his left hand up to steady the gun while simultaneously batting the barrel with his right. The barrel snapped and clinked into the gutter. An incredulous expression spread over the gunman's round face.

"Yeah," Remo repeated. "I'm in a bad mood."

The gunman tried to fire anyway, but Remo's hand was a vise preventing the cylinder from turning. Then Remo took the gun and popped the cylinder out of its frame. He dropped the ruined weapon.

That was enough for the gunman, who slid back across the seat and hit the gas. Remo swept out a leg and clipped the right rear tire with a toe as hard as a crowbar. The tire blew.

The car kept going, however, but not as fast as its driver would have liked. The wrecked tire wobbled crazily and dragged. Turning a corner, the wheel rim sheared through the rubber.

Remo caught up to the car and ran along with it.

"Get away from me!" the driver yelled.

"Tell you what," Remo said as he jogged beside him. "I could use some exercise. You're going to be the ball."

Remo sped forward and cut in front of the car. Just for effect he took out the headlights with two quick jabs. Then he got to the other side and with a sharp kick made the left front tire let go. The car slowed considerably, and stopped altogether when Remo ruptured the right front tire.

The gunman hastily rolled up his window as Remo sauntered back to the driver's side and took out the remaining tire. For good measure, he popped the trunk open with the flat of a palm and rolled out the spare. A finger thrust rendered the spare useless.

There was a jack in the trunk, and it gave Remo an idea. He grabbed it and set it up under the chassis, taking a moment to methodically destroy all the locks on the doors so the driver could not escape, and then jacked one side of the car up as far as it would go.

It was far enough so that Remo could take the chassis in

both hands and, coming to his feet from a kneeling position, flip the car slowly onto its roof.

The roof crumpled. The driver screamed.

At that point a knot of pedestrians gathered.

They watched as Remo, seemingly playing the part of a good samaritan, knocked out the window glass on the driver's side.

"Are you all right, pal?" Remo asked.

The driver was all but standing on his head and had a gusher of a nosebleed that rampaged down into his eyes.

"Get me out of here! Get me out!"

"Scared?" Remo asked solicitously.

"Yeah, yeah—get me out!"

"Want not to be scared?"

"Yeah—yeah, I do."

So Remo shot a hard finger into the man's forehead, which cancelled out his emotions. Not to mention his life.

"Your wish is granted," Remo said.

"Is he going to be all right?" someone asked as Remo walked off.

"Sure is. I gave him first aid."

The FOES office was still empty when Remo got there, but he was in a better mood. Chiun had always said that exercise was good for the spirit as well as the body. Thinking of Chiun again, Remo felt a twinge.

It was time for a long talk with Chiun.

Not fearing attack, the Master of Sinanju hadn't bothered to lock the door. Remo just walked in.

Chiun, attired in the white kimono that he seldom wore, sat writing on a piece of parchment. He did not acknowledge Remo, although Remo knew Chiun was aware of his presence.

"I have come to talk, Little Father," Remo said quietly in Korean.

"I have offended you, I know," Remo said, finding the words more difficult than expected. He cleared his throat.

"If this is the end of our travels together," Remo said, "then I will accept that fact if I must. It is not my wish to put our friendship aside, but if it is your wish, then my respect for you forces me to accept this."

Chiun gave no sign he heard, but his pen scratched less furiously.

"But just as I have my respect for you, you must respect me. I am prepared to say my last good-bye and wish to atone for my offense before we part. But because I do not know how I have offended you, I cannot do this. You must tell me. This is my parting request to you, who have been both parent and teacher to me."

When Chiun finally spoke, it was after a long silence, and he did not look up from his writing.

"That was a good speech, excellently spoken," he said tonelessly.

"Thank you," Remo said, a lump growing in his throat. *Dammit! Why do I feel like this?* he asked himself.

"But your voice broke toward the last," Chiun added, and resumed his writing. A long silence stretched into minutes in which neither of them spoke.

"Sit at my feet, Remo," Chiun said at last.

Remo sat, his face a mask.

"Emperor Smith has been trying to reach you."

"I don't care about Smith," Remo said.

"And your assignment? Do you no longer care about that?"

"I don't know," Remo said truthfully.

"Then what do you care about?" Chiun dropped his quill for the first time and faced Remo. His expression was unreadable.

"I care about you. I care about us."

Chiun nodded and turned his parchment over.

"Do you remember the legend of the Great Master Wang?" Chiun asked.

"There are many legends about Wang," Remo replied.

"True. But one stands above all other." Chiun placed

his hands flat on his lap and spoke with his eyes closed, as if from memory.

"There is a saying in my village, 'Blue comes from indigo but is bluer.' This means that a pupil can sometimes exceed his Master. So it was with Wang in the long-ago days of Sinanju. Now, Wang was not the first of the Masters of Sinanju. No, many came before him, and many came after, and some who followed also took the name of Wang.

"Before Wang, the Master was named Hung. A good Master was Hung, and the last of the old Masters of Sinanju, who knew not the sun source. In those days the Master was followed by lesser Masters, who were known as night tigers.

"When the time came for Hung to train his replacement, he chose a young night tiger named Wang, who was my ancestor. Wang was not a difficult choice, for in the years those times were hard, and the babies of Wang's generation had mostly been sent home to the sea. Those who survived were not always healthy, although some made adequate night tigers. But only Wang, Hung saw, was worthy to train as the next Master, and Wang began that training, quickly proving himself an apt student and possessive of the promise of true leadership.

"But, woe, before Wang had been training more than one year, the Master Hung died in his sleep. There was no shame attached to this, Remo, for this Master was still young, being only seventy-five. Yet he died before his time, leaving no heir worthy of being called the Master of Sinanju. This tragedy had never before happened to the House of Sinanju."

Remo had heard this story before, but listened patiently.

"And the people of the village gathered around the body of Hung," Chiun continued. "And with much wailing and weeping, they consigned his body to the earth, setting a marker upon it which said: HERE LIES HUNG, THE LAST MASTER OF SINANJU.

"And so it seemed. The glory of the finest house of assassins the world had ever nurtured was no more.

"The people of Sinanju huddled by their fires, for winter was fast approaching, and they asked themselves, 'What are we to do now that there is no Master to protect us and feed our bellies and our children's bellies?'

"And some said, 'We will have to send the babies home to the sea again.'

" 'But there are so few babies even now,' said others.

" 'Perhaps we should leave this wretched village for the south.'

" 'Oh, woe,' they cried. 'To no longer be Sinanju. To no longer be above all others. If only Hung had not died too soon. If only Wang had learned more.'

"And so they grieved and complained to one another, not one of them offering any solution to their plight. And Wang, young and beset by the guilt the others had forced upon him, went off with his thoughts to the hills east of Sinanju.

"There he meditated for five days. Although he had been taught proper diet, Wang ate only rice hulls and grass roots because he wished to purge his mind of all distraction. After three days, he forebore all food and concentrated on proper breathing alone, an art which was known then, although not refined.

"After five days, Wang's meditation bore no fruit. He had no solution to Sinanju's grave plight. Further, his spirit was failing for he was weak from hunger and very cold. In truth, life and will were slipping from his body.

"On the fifth night, he lay on his back staring into the heavens. Above him, the stars moved inexorably, and it seemed to Wang they were cold, uncaring stars, unmindful of the tragedy gathering on the shores of the West Korean Bay. Yet at the same time Wang could see that the stars never went out; they were always burning, just like the sun. If only people could burn as bright and as long . . . Wang thought.

"It was then a great ring of fire came down from the skies. The fire had a message for Wang. It said that men do not use their minds and bodies as they should; they wasted their spirit and strength. The ring of fire taught Wang the lessons of control—and though Wang's enlightenment came in a single burst of flame, his mastery of what he had learned took a lifetime.

"This was the beginning of the sun source," Chiun finished, opening his clear eyes.

"You think there is some connection between that ring of fire and these UFOs?" Remo asked, frowning.

"The sun source is known," Chiun said slowly. "But the source of the sun source is not known. Many Masters have contemplated the mystery of the ring of fire which spoke to Wang, for it is the greatest mystery of Sinanju. I myself have given this much thought. And you, Remo?"

Remo shrugged. "I thought it was just a legend."

"I see. Then perhaps you are not responsible after all."

"I'm not?" Remo asked hopefully.

"When I first read of these USOs, Remo, I saw in their mystery the answer to the greatest riddle of Sinanju. It was no accident that we of Sinanju, in the hour of our direst need, were given the gift of the sun source. A wiser power from the stars saw that our glory should not fade from this earth, and perhaps one of their USOs visited with Wang and through their skill placed the secret of the sun source into his brain.

"If this were true, then it is the duty of the Master of Sinanju to make contact with the descendants of the Master who gave Sinanju to the Greatest Master Wang. For we are bound by a common destiny."

"Let me get this straight," Remo said. "You think

the things we can do with our bodies are because a flying saucer dropped in on Wang?''

"An emissary from an advanced Korean civilization," Chiun corrected.

"Korean? How do you figure Korean?"

"Very simple. Korean is the most civilized nation on this planet. It therefore follows that any advanced people on other planets are Korean, too. Besides, this Master from the House of Beetle Goose has a Korean name. He told it to me."

"He did? What is it?"

"Well," Chiun said evasively. "He pronounced it differently than you and I would. His accent was atrocious."

"Right. But what was his name?"

"He called himself Hopak Kay," Chiun said quickly.

"Hopak Kay? What does it mean?"

"It does not matter what it means. It is his name."

Remo scratched his head. Hopak Kay? The words sounded familiar, but Remo's command of Korean was not exactly fluent.

"What is important," Chiun continued, "is that I had made contact with this Master."

"And I screwed it up?"

"Yes, you screwed it up."

"I did not know, Little Father. I am sorry."

"Are you prepared to atone for this?" Chiun asked.

"If it is within my power," Remo replied.

"Then you will help me regain contact with this World Master?"

"Does that mean I'm forgiven?"

"Yes, Remo. I forgive you."

"Thank you, Little Father," Remo said gratefully. He no longer felt like an orphan. "It was my speech that did it, wasn't it?"

Chiun smiled. "Yes, it was your beautiful speech which touched my heart." And Chiun tore to pieces the parchment on which he had been writing, pleased that he had been spared the necessity of finishing the long letter in which he told Remo that despite all the insults and indignities he had suffered, Chiun would return to resume Remo's training since Remo was of such a level of ineptitude that without Chiun, he was in danger of being run over by a three-wheeled bicycle.

CHAPTER THIRTEEN

"I'd better check in with Smitty," Remo said, picking up the telephone. "What did he say he wanted?"

"He wanted you to recover something that was stolen from your country," Chiun said absently.

"Oh yeah? Did he say what it was?"

"It was one of those ridiculous atomic things."

"What! You mean an atomic bomb?" Remo demanded.

"No, not one of those."

"Good," Remo said, listening to the Folcroft number ring.

"Smith called it a warhead," Chiun remarked.

"An atomic warhead's been stolen!" Remo shouted.

"Yes, I know, Remo," Smith's lemony voice came over the receiver. "I've been trying to reach you about it. And there's no need to shout. I can hear perfectly."

"Smitty, what's going on?"

"Not good, Remo. The Air Force secretly moved the damaged Titan missile today, along with its warhead, which took a different route for security reasons. The vehicle carrying the warhead disappeared en route, and its driver was found dead. He'd apparently been left, unconscious, on a road three miles from the missile base, where he was run over."

"In other words, you don't know who took this thing?"

"No, but it's safe to assume that the same group who

131

sabotaged the Titan in the first place is responsible. Can you make contact with them again?"

"I'll try. Is the warhead alive?"

"Unfortunately, yes. It couldn't be deactivated on site. The damage to the missile precluded that. Remo, I don't have to tell you how serious this is. You'll have to find a way to bring Chiun back into this."

"I already have, Smitty," Remo said coolly.

"Good," said Smith, moving on to the next order of business. "You must locate the warhead as soon as possible. When you do, contact me immediately."

"Don't you want to know how I convinced Chiun to—"

"No," Smith said, and hung up.

"Those crazy flying saucer people have ripped off a live warhead," Remo informed Chiun.

"Yes, I believe they said something about ridding the world of those insane devices. I do not think that is so crazy."

"That depends on whether one goes off in their faces or not. They've been lucky so far. We've got to find them, and when we do we'll find that UFO, too."

"I will go put on an appropriate kimono," Chiun said.

When he returned, the Master of Sinanju wore a green ceremonial robe on which twin peacocks strutted. "Am I presentable?" he asked.

"Only if they're hiding at a circus," Remo said, but he smiled.

Chiun smiled back. Things were back to normal.

At Chiun's insistence Remo drove to FOES headquarters, even though he had been there earlier and found nothing.

"Emptiness is always temporary," Chiun pointed out.

The door was ajar when they got there, and sounds came from inside.

"Let's take him, whoever it is," Remo suggested.

"No," Chiun said. "We will wish to follow this person to our goal. Let us be unobtrusive."

"You'll have to leave the building for that," Remo remarked, eyeing the peacocks on Chiun's robe.

But they both melted into the shadows in time to avoid being seen by Pavel Zarnitsa, who was anxious to locate the farm of a certain Ethel Sump.

"Who was he?" Remo asked after he had gone.

"I did not recognize him," Chiun admitted. "He is not one of the group belonging to the blonde woman with the cavernous mouth."

"We'll follow him anyway. He's all we've got."

They let their quarry reach his rented car before they started theirs. Remo followed at a discreet distance, which was not a problem. The leading car gave off a noxious exhaust, which Remo's sensitive nostrils could follow from better than a mile.

"Good. He's going south, Chiun."

But the Master of Sinanju was too engrossed to reply. He was busy solving his Rubik's Cube for what Remo thought must have been the hundredth time.

"Haven't you gotten tired of that thing yet?" he complained.

"One does not tire of new challenges," Chiun sniffed.

"What new challenges?" Remo demanded. "You've already broken the record on that thing twice."

"But I have not solved the puzzle with my eyes closed."

"Hah! And you're not going to, either. I still haven't figured out how you do it, but no one can do it with their eyes closed."

"No?" Chiun inquired. "Watch."

And while Remo watched out of the corner of his eye, Chiun went through an elaborate series of motions like a magician proving that he had nothing hidden up his sleeve. Then he raised the cube from his lap and, tightly closing his eyes, solved the puzzle in a blur of colored squares and flying fingers.

"There. A new way. Perhaps I should go on television."

Remo bit his tongue and concentrated on the road ahead. The thick smell of exhaust fumes made him want to gag. Chiun, immensely pleased with himself, took a nap and promptly began snoring.

"Large hairy dog!"

Chiun snapped awake in mid-snore. "What is wrong, Remo? What is it?"

"Large hairy dog," Remo repeated triumphantly. "I've been trying to remember it for the last twenty minutes. Hopak Kay means 'large hairy dog' in Korean. This alien's name is Large Hairy Dog!"

Chiun's face assumed an embarrassed expression. "Do not make light of another's name. In the culture from which he comes, it is no doubt a proud and worthy name. You should take that into account."

"Since when are you so understanding of other cultures?"

"I have always been that way," Chiun insisted.

"Try to keep that in mind the next time you want me to grow Fu Manchu fingernails."

Pavel Zarnitsa found the farmhouse that should have belonged to Ethel Sump, drove well past it, and pulled off the road. He quietly assembled his plastic pistol and walked back in the direction of the farm, with its weeds and weatherbeaten barn.

He did not pay any attention to the car that shot past him, and so did not know that it, too, parked not far down the road.

The farm was so run-down, it made Pavel a little sick when he got to it. In Russia, such neglect was practically treasonous. How did they feed people with such waste? Thinking of food made Pavel's mouth water. He would enjoy a taco very much right about now.

There was a light in one window, and Pavel went toward it in a sort of crouching run. He waited in the darkness until he was satisfied that his movements had gone unnoticed. And when he peered into the house, there was no sign of people except for the light, which showed a rather unkempt parlor.

Making a circuit of the place, Pavel discovered the van, which told him that someone had to be there. He was about to investigate the barn when a weird thing happened.

The barn began to glow.

The barn had been a dark shape against some feathery redbud trees and looked ready to fall over in a stiff wind. There were missing boards and a ragged hole in the roof. Suddenly, a tremendous white light seemed to fill the barn and leak from the chinks and holes. There were a lot of these, so it made the barn all but glow.

A long, eerie sigh came from within, like a chorus of awestruck worshipers at the Second Coming.

Pavel crept toward the light, this time on his stomach. What he saw through a knothole made him forget all about his appetite.

He saw a round metallic object of many bright lights, which began to change color before his startled eye. The object floated in the exact center of the barn. It wobbled slightly, but otherwise did not move. It made no sound. It was a fantastic sight.

There were also people inside the barn. Switching eyes because of the intense light, Pavel saw that they looked human. There seemed to be about ten of them, led by a tall blonde woman in some kind of black uniform. The others were also in black, including one who hobbled on crutches, and another who knelt before the floating object. This man was not in black, and the blonde leader held a gun to his head.

"He says his name is Thad Screiber, and he claims he's a

reporter," the blonde said loudly. It was clear she was speaking to the weird object.

When the object replied in an unearthly voice, Pavel felt his flesh crawl a little.

"You have moved the warhead to a safe location, Preparation Group Leader?" the voice demanded unemotionally.

"Two of our people are guarding it now," Amanda Bull said.

"We are then at a dangerous juncture in our plans to dismantle America's nuclear arsenal."

Dismantle America's nuclear arsenal? Pavel thought incredulously. And what was this about a warhead?

"What do we do with this reporter, World Master?" Amanda asked. "He followed us here and could wreck everything. Should I shoot him? I wouldn't mind."

This brought some grumblings of discontent from the others in the group. The reporter swayed a little on his knees. He looked a little green, but that might have been the lights.

"Quiet!" Amanda snapped at the others.

"No, shooting him will accomplish nothing," the strange voice spoke.

Everyone looked relieved, including Thad Screiber. He shut his eyes in relief and so did not see the blue needle of light suddenly stab from the UFO and impale him for a moment in eternity. The beam went completely through him at a downward angle and started a small fire on the ground behind him. Thad Screiber fell back into the tiny flames, and his dead body smothered those flames.

"But demonstrating my power will," the World Master intoned. "Have some of you forgotten the gravity of our work? If so, then consider this: you have participated in the theft of one of your nation's most dangerous and important weapons. In the eyes of your people, you are all traitors. Only by continuing along the path I have marked and creating a new world order can you escape capture and execution. No one must stand in our way.''

The barn held a long silence in which beautiful light played along its walls and on the faces of its stunned occupants. Even Amanda Bull was shocked by the stern tone of the World Master. She recovered her composure long enough to say, "Preparation Group Number Two stands ready to fulfill its glorious destiny.''

"Excellent," the reedy voice commented. "And your destiny *will* be glorious, I promise you. In the new world, you will all be giants. Future generations will sing your praises. But first, we must insure that there will be a future for your tiny planet, which is my planet's mission.''

"Orders?" Amanda asked stiffly.

"You will transport the Titan warhead to the center of the population area known as Oklahoma City and detonate it.''

Amanda swallowed hard. Ethel Sump fainted, and the others looked as if they wanted to. Pavel Zarnitsa felt none too good himself. From what he could piece together, it sounded very much as if World War III was about to be started by a bunch of Americans, on orders from a being from another planet!

And there was no doubt in his mind that if Oklahoma City should be obliterated, America's nuclear finger would swiftly be pointed to Soviet Russia.

Pavel knew he couldn't allow that. He was about to move from where he crouched when the barn doors were flung open and a strident voice announced, "Hail all! The Master of the House of Sinanju brings greetings to the Master of the House of Beetle Goose!''

Chiun, resplendent in his green ceremonial robes, strode boldly into the startled group. Remo, more wary, stood at his side.

Amanda Bull whipped her gun up toward Chiun but Remo cleared the distance between them before a shot could be fired, and suddenly Amanda was staring at her empty gun hand, which stung painfully.

Remo extracted the clip, cleared the chamber, and tossed the weapon aside.

"You won't be needing that," he told her.

"Yes," Chiun called out, "no violence is necessary. We have come in peace. We have come to resume ties with the House of Beetle Goose."

"If you have come here with peaceful intent," the World Master said, "then speak."

"There has been a misunderstanding between our houses, World Master," Chiun said. "I wish a private audience."

"As proof of your peaceful intent, you will allow your companion to be held prisoner during your audience."

"Done," Chiun said. "Remo, return the woman's weapon."

"Chiun, I don't like this. These clowns were just talking about blowing up Oklahoma City."

"Remo!" Chiun said sharply.

Remo reluctantly returned the automatic to Amanda, who quickly rammed home a fresh clip.

"All right, I've got you, buster!" Amanda crowed.

"Good for you," Remo said sourly. He was looking around for the man they had tailed here. Now where could he be?

Chiun entered the ship of the World Master through a panel, which quickly shut after him. He stood again within the outer chamber, which suddenly filled with a golden light. It was a very peaceful light, Chiun thought.

When the shadow of the World Master crossed the pebbled-glass screen, Chiun bowed low.

"My ancestors smile upon this meeting," Chiun said quietly.

"And mine," returned the World Master.

"I have many questions," Chiun began.

"And your persistence has earned you the right to many answers."

"Many generations ago, one of my ancestors met with one of your people. In the hour of his greatest need, when even life itself was failing, a ring of fire descended from the heavens and a voice was heard."

"Yes, my voice."

Chiun's beard trembled. "Yours?"

"Yes. My life span is greater than you could imagine."

"Truly, then, I stand in the presence of a great Master. For it was you who made my people what they are today."

"This is correct. Far, far in your planet's past, my world saw that this Earth held great potential. We came in our ships and with our science, propelled the apes and the monkeys on the upward evolutionary path that led to your humans."

"Apes? Monkeys?" Chiun said bewilderedly. "You must be referring to some other things. My Korean ancestors do not come from mere apes. I have been taught that our line sprang from the pairing of the great Tangun and a bear."

"Yes, this is true," the World Master said. "I am Tangun."

This time Chiun's entire body trembled. "You? Tangun? You have told me that your name is Hopak Kay."

"My full name is Tangun Hopak Kay."

"That is a strange name," said Chiun slowly.

"To human ears perhaps."

"Tell me of your world," Chiun asked next. "I wish to know more of it."

"It is a world of beauty and peace, which I know you would find to your liking. There is no hate, no crime, no wars. This is the image in which I intend to remake your world. One devoid of ugliness and evil. Where all men will live in true harmony, and the old will be cherished in their declining years."

"Yes, that will be good for them," Chiun said absently. "But tell me more. Tell me of the sun source."

"On my world as well as yours, the sun is a great source of energy. But we have learned to harness that energy more efficiently. All things on my planet are solar-powered."

Chiun's hazel eyes narrowed to slits. "And your assassins. What of them?"

"My civilization long ago advanced beyond such practices. The last of our assassins were rehabilitated through brain operations. They were rendered meek and nonviolent in this manner."

"You have answered all my questions," the Master of Sinanju announced suddenly. "I wish to confer with my son."

"You may do this," the World Master said, and the panel reopened. "But you must both decide if you wish to join with me in my plan to eradicate war and the evils of assassination after that."

Chiun left the gently bobbing ship.

When Pavel Zarnitsa saw that everyone in the barn was distracted by the reappearance of the old Oriental from the UFO—or whatever it was—he decided it was time to make his move.

He dashed inside, waved his pistol for all to see, and shouted at the top of his lungs, "You will all stand perfectly still, please! You, drop your weapon," Pavel told Amanda, who complied hastily. "The rest of you stand aside. I am claiming this spacecraft and its secrets on behalf of my government!"

"*You fool, Pavel Zarnitsa! You will ruin everything!*" The voice of the World Master was an amplified screech.

Pavel almost dropped his weapon in shock.

"You . . . you know my name?" Pavel demanded. "Who? How?"

"*You have ruined everything,*" the voice said, and then a low humming filled the barn.

"Chiun! There's that sound again," Remo shouted, expecting his skin to heat up.

But it didn't. Instead, there came a sputtering and hissing from within the floating object, which suddenly fell to the ground. White-hot sparks like the product of a dozen arc-welding torches spilled out of the object. They hurt the eyes and caused everyone to look away in pain. Smoke filled the barn. People ran and collided with one another.

Remo, shielding his eyes, tried to find Chiun in the confusion. "Little Father," he shouted, "where—"

"Hush, Remo. I am here."

Remo felt a familiar hand take his. Chiun, seemingly oblivious to the smoke and sputtering light, guided them both away from the barn, which had started to blaze.

Remo glanced back once and saw the UFO. It was partially obscured by the smoke, but he clearly saw it slowly melting into a puddle of incandescent slag. There was no sign of the being who called himself the World Master.

CHAPTER FOURTEEN

"Over here," Remo was saying. "I found one."

"One what?" Chiun called from inside the smoldering barn. The structure had burned almost to the ground before the fire had gone out on its own. Parts of two sides still stood stubbornly.

"One of the ones who didn't get away," Remo said, looking down at the stunned figure of Pavel Zarnitsa, whose face was black with soot.

"He—he knew my name," Pavel said dazedly. "How could he know my name?"

Remo, noticing his captive's accent, demanded, "You sound like a Russian."

"I am a Polack," Pavel told him, sitting up.

"Yeah? Well I've been to Russia, and I know what a Russian sounds like. And for my money, buddy, you sound like a Russian to me."

"Have you ever been to Poland?"

"Uh . . . no," Remo admitted.

"Then I submit you do not know what you are speaking of."

"Hey, Chiun, come listen to this guy. I think he's a Russian," Remo shouted.

"I do not have to listen to him," Chiun called back. "I can smell him. He is a Russian."

"I knew it," Remo said, lifting Pavel to his feet with one hand. "Time to come clean."

Pavel reached for his pistol, but Remo got to it first. He squeezed hard, and the weapon fell in pieces from his hand.

"Pretty neat trick, right?" Remo said.

"No," Pavel said. "Anyone could do it. The weapon is plastic."

"I'm beginning not to like you," Remo told him.

"That is too bad for one of us," Pavel admitted unhappily.

"You got that right," Remo said, dragging the Russian over to where Chiun picked through what was left of the UFO.

There wasn't much left—surprisingly little for such a large object, in fact. Most of it was shiny slag—a bit like a large bob of lead that had been melted down—only whatever the metal had been, it wasn't lead, and it was still too hot to touch. There were other things, too. Pieces of machinery that had been inside the UFO. Some of these stuck out of the smooth slag like jagged teeth, but even these had withered in the intense heat.

"If there's any body inside that mess," Remo ventured, "it must have been burned to the size of a dog. A small dog, at that."

"There is no body," Chiun spat.

"You think this World Master escaped with the rest of them?" Remo asked.

"Of course," Chiun returned, folding his hands within his sleeves. "The others could not have escaped on their own. Someone led them. Someone who was not the blonde woman."

"Why not her?" asked Remo.

"Because someone who would let a tiny hair grow on the bridge of her nose could not successfully lead others to safety," Chiun told him.

"Right," Remo said, looking around. "Well, it's obvious they got away in the van—all except this guy, here."

"I am not one of those people," Pavel pointed out.

"I'll bet," Remo said.

"He is telling the truth," Chiun said. "I do not recognize him as a follower of the blonde woman. Nor do I recognize the body of the white you so foolishly tried to rescue."

"I didn't know he was dead when I went back in to get him," Remo protested.

"If you had not gone back into the fire, I would not have had to go back also to protect you, and the others would not have escaped."

"I'm sorry, Little Father. I know how much you value making contact with this Hopak Kay."

Chiun spat on the ground violently. "Pah! He is well named. He is a dog and son of dog."

"What's that?" Remo asked quizzically.

"Nothing," Chiun muttered, and stormed off.

Remo turned to the Russian. "And where do you fit into this?"

Pavel Zarnitsa shrugged his shoulders and his bushy eyebrows at the same time. "I am just a Polack passerby."

"No, you're not. We followed you here. How are you connected with these flying-saucer chasers?"

Pavel saw no harm in answering that question, so he did.

"I was chasing them," he said.

"Why?"

"To see to what they were up, just as you were. Where is the harm in that?"

"We're Americans. You aren't," Remo said simply.

"That does not mean I have no interest in keeping America from destroying itself."

"America isn't trying to destroy itself," Remo said.

"But some Americans are," Pavel countered. "We have both witnessed this. There is a nuclear device that has fallen into their hands, and into the spaceman's hands."

"How do you know he's a spaceman?"

Pavel paled slightly in the darkness so that Remo noticed. "He knew my name. He spoke it. How could he know this? No one knows I am here. Not even my superiors.'' His voice was unsteady. ''He can read minds, perhaps?''

Remo didn't know the answer to that. Chiun believed that the alien was genuine, and connected to Sinanju. Chiun wasn't always right, but Remo had never known him to make a mistake where Sinanju was concerned. Maybe he could read minds.

''You said something about your superiors,'' Remo said suddenly. ''Who?''

''I cannot tell you that,'' Pavel insisted.

''Yes, you can. You just need incentive. Incentive is an American idea, but I'll be glad to show you how it works.''

Remo took Pavel Zarnitsa by the left earlobe and squeezed. It looked as if Remo were just being playful, but then the Russian's expression warped like heated wax, and his knees buckled. Remo lifted, and the Russian obligingly stood on tiptoe. He did not fight, even though his hands were free.

Instead, he said, ''Oooch! Yow! Oooch!'' several times very fast, and finished by admitting, ''KGB! I am KGB!''

''What else?''

''I am not in your beautiful country to spy on you. I am here to keep an eye on Russians. I like America. Honestly. My favorite American food is tacos.''

Remo squeezed harder.

''I read about your missiles, so I come here to see what trouble you are having. I learn enough to come here, and to know that what is happening is not good. Not good for Russians or Americans. So you see, we are on the same side, no?''

Remo let Pavel loose, knowing he had been telling the truth.

''We are on the same side, definitely no,'' Remo said. He walked over to the body of Thad Screiber, which lay blackened and singed on the ground. Remo forced his pupils to dilate so he could see the dead man's face in the darkness. Somewhere a bird called twice.

"Know this guy?" Remo asked Pavel.

"No. But they said he was a reporter who learned too much. The spaceman zipped him."

"Did what?"

"Zipped him," Pavel repeated. "Like in your science fiction movies. There was a beam of blue light. Then he fell over dead. Look. There will be a hole."

Remo looked. The hole was there. Not large, but it went clean through. The wound was even cauterized. Some kind of death beam, Remo realized.

"He got zapped, all right," Remo admitted. He found a wallet on the body, which identified him as Thad Screiber, of Northfield, Minnesota. Other than that, Remo could learn nothing about him. There was no indication that he belonged to the Oklahoma City chapter of FOES. Or any other chapter, for that matter. That probably meant he was what he had claimed to be, a reporter.

Remo found Chiun inside the farmhouse. There was a body there, too. A woman's.

"She was one of them," Chiun said.

"Yeah, I recognize her," Remo said. "She was the one the blonde shot by accident that first time when she tried to shoot me. Looks like they dragged her back here, and she died."

"The body is still warm," Chiun said. "Had they sought medical attention, she might have been saved."

"Anyway, we've got to find what's left of the group before they do more damage. The question is, where do we look?"

"Look at maps," Pavel suggested.

"What maps?" Remo demanded.

"Any maps. They always leave maps around. They are very careless. This is how I know to come here. They left a map in their office. They left names and addresses. Perhaps they do the same here.''

''I was in that office twice and didn't find anything,'' Remo said.

Pavel shrugged his shoulders in time with his eyebrows. ''You are not properly trained.''

''You are smart for a stupid Russian,'' Chiun remarked.

Remo gave them both a look, but he searched the place anyway. The trouble was that he didn't know what he was looking for. He never had been much good at this sort of thing. It was a lot easier when Smith did all the rooting around and just told Remo who the hit was, what he looked like and where to find him.

As a consequence of his preoccupation, Remo found nothing and said so.

''There's nothing here.''

''Now I will try,'' Pavel Zarnitsa offered. He ignored every area Remo had already checked, simply because he had watched Remo go through the house and knew there was nothing of worth to be found in those places. Remo had been looking for hidden materials. Pavel knew that the FOES group did not hide things. They were not that well-trained or that smart. Consequently, they had out-smarted Remo.

''Here,'' Pavel said, returning from the kitchen. He had a notepad on which someone had been doodling. In among the doodles were two words, ''Broken Arrow.''

Remo read the pad. ''Doesn't mean anything to me. Better call Smith.''

''Who's Smith?'' Pavel asked.

The look Remo and Chiun gave him made Pavel wish very, very much that he had not asked that question.

''I will wait in the next room while you talk,'' Pavel offered.

Despite the late hour, Remo got Smith immediately. Remo rattled off the events of the evening as fast as he could. "The only clue we found," he finished, "is a notepad. Someone wrote Broken Arrow on it."

"Anything else?" Smith asked.

"No. It's stuck in the middle of some doodles, but they aren't anything."

"Broken Arrow is a code designation for a serious nuclear accident," Smith said. "The code for a lesser incident is Bent Spear."

"Then it's just someone scribbling on a notepad," Remo suggested.

"There's also a town named Broken Arrow in Oklahoma. Near Tulsa, I think."

"Then we'd better check it out," Remo said.

"No. You told me you overheard the individual called the World Master issue instructions to place the warhead in Oklahoma City for detonation. You must go there first. Finding that device is everything now, Remo. The newspapers know about the Titan accident now."

"I thought they already did," Remo said.

"They had rumors. But I just had information that the *New York Times* is about to break an eyewitness account of the missile salvage operation. Evidently, a reporter named . . ." Smith paused and Remo heard a rustle of papers. ". . . Thad Screiber managed to get close to the operation. I don't know where he fits in."

"He doesn't anymore," Remo said. "He's here. Dead. They killed him."

"That may be good," Smith decided. "If this whole story gets out, it will galvanize the antinuclear people. They're apt to go overboard and demand we dismantle our defensive missile program."

"Yeah. Well, that's your worry, Smitty. I'm going to have my hands full finding that warhead and handling Chiun at the same time." Remo lowered his voice and glanced sideways at Chiun, who was peeking into the next room to make sure the Russian wasn't eavesdropping. "Chiun is convinced this World Master had something to do with his ancestors. It's too complicated to explain now, but Chiun wants to be friends with him.''

"Chiun believes this person is what he claims to be?"

"Yeah. Maybe I do, too. I don't know. But I do know if it comes down to a choice between Oklahoma City and not antagonizing him, I'd get ready to order a new set of wall maps.''

"Hmmm," Smith mused. "Perhaps I'd better recall Chiun to Folcroft. Tell him the sun is setting in the east.''

"Huh? It's not—"

"That's the code for him to return on his own.''

"Oh," Remo said. "Hey, Chiun, Smith says to tell you that the sun is setting in the east.''

"Tell Emperor Smith he does not have to worry," Chiun called back. "The Master of Sinanju will return when he has finished the Emperor's business.''

"You heard him," Remo told Smith. "He's not budging.''

"Very well," Smith said grimly. "I'm going to count on you, Remo. You must not fail. Locate the warhead and inform me immediately. I'll take care of the rest.''

"What about this Russian?"

"Did you get his name?"

"No. Never thought to ask," Remo said. He called into the next room. "Hey, buddy, you got a name?"

"Ivan Vobla," Pavel called back.

"His name is Pavel Zarnitsa," Chiun spat. "I heard him called that.''

"Yeah, that's right," Remo said. "This World Master recognized him right off. Called him by name. He can't figure it out himself. He keeps babbling about it.''

"Remo, are you sure?" Smith demanded.

"Yeah, I am. Why?"

"I don't know," Smith said slowly. "Let me check my files." There was a pause while Smith called up some information on his computer.

"Yes, I do have a Pavel Zarnitsa. KGB. Currently stationed in New York City to monitor Russian employees working for *Aeroflot*. Extremely few people know he is in America. . . .''

"So what do I do with him?"

"I don't know where he fits in, but hold on to him. Better yet, tell Chiun that he is responsible for Zarnitsa. That may keep him from interfering with your movements."

Remo looked over and saw Chiun and the Russian giving each other looks of mutual dislike.

"I'm sure they're both going to be very happy with your decision," Remo said before he hung up.

CHAPTER FIFTEEN

Amanda Bull was beginning to wonder. She had had questions before, but the World Master had always answered them, and the answers had always dispelled her worries. She had had doubts before, but they were little doubts, and they always went away when she stopped thinking of them.

They didn't go away this time.

All during the ride back to Oklahoma City, she had questions and doubts. She could understand that there might be a reason for the World Master's spacecraft to suddenly disintegrate. A malfunction, for instance. Unavoidable, perhaps. She could understand the need to evacuate everyone. There was the danger from Remo, and then the strange man with the gun and the thick accent. Who had he been? And why did the World Master shout that he had ruined everything? There were probably answers to those questions, too. Good, sensible, logical answers. Of that, Amanda had little doubt.

What really disturbed Amanda did not strike her until after she and the rest of the Preparation Group had been led from the burning barn by the World Master himself. He had seemingly materialized out of the sparks and flames and smoke to take Amanda's hand and lead her out of the blaze through a hole between two boards. The others had followed while Remo and the Oriental were trying to escape themselves. It had been dark, and no one could see very clearly. Except the World Master. It had been he who made them all link hands and who led them to the waiting van. It had been he who had ordered the others to take the van, while pushing himself and Amanda into that reporter's car, which was parked nearby, and instructed them all to drive as fast as possible to Oklahoma City. All that made sense, and so Amanda followed orders as she always did.

But what was strange, and what did not hit home until they were on the road and clearly going to escape pursuit, was that the World Master seemed to have no trouble breathing in the Earth's atmosphere.

Amanda looked into the rearview mirror for the sixth time. Even in the darkness of a country road she could see that the individual who occupied the rear seat of the car was not wearing a helmet of any kind. He didn't have a breathing mask, either. That was clear. As for the face of the World Master, it had frightened Amanda horribly the first time she had looked into the mirror, and she almost lost control of the car. But, as if she were at a freak show, she couldn't resist another look, and then still another, until the shadowy face hovering behind her in the dark seemed like an image out of a horror movie—scary, but familiar.

"Can—can you breathe okay?" Amanda asked.

The voice that answered was no longer thin and high, but a sinister baritone. It said:

"Be silent, stupid woman. You have failed miserably."

"But . . . I *tried*," Amanda wailed.

"And failed. There is no excuse. I should not have entrusted such responsibility to a mere woman."

"Mere . . . But you said that—"

"I said be silent!"

And Amanda began to cry.

"Stop this vehicle, Remo," the Master of Sinanju demanded.

"Now? Chiun, we've got to catch these people before they get to the city."

"I no longer wish to sit back here with this Russian pervert," Chiun spat.

"Then climb over the seat."

"I will not climb over the seat like a child. Stop this car so that one may change his seat with dignity."

Remo braked the car. Chiun, gathering his robes about him, stepped out of the back and took the seat next to Remo, who got going again.

"Oklahoma City is about to be blown to chalk dust, and you have to change seats," Remo complained.

Chiun sniffed. "Emperor Smith may have entrusted this Russian prisoner to my keeping, but that does not mean I am forced to listen to a recitation of his filthy habits."

"What filthy habits?" Remo asked, eyeing Pavel Zarnitsa in the rearview mirror. Zarnitsa looked sheepish sitting all by himself.

"His filthy eating habits," Chiun told him.

Pavel, hearing this, leaned forward eagerly and protested. "I have not filthy habits," he insisted. "I was simply discussing my appreciation for that wonderful American delicacy, the taco."

Chiun made a disgusted noise.

"Tacos?" Remo said in surprise.

"Yes, they are some horrible food made with meat and spices," Chiun explained to Remo.

"I know what they are," Remo said. "I just never heard anyone call them a delicacy before."

"Well, they are not. And if this Russian's description is accurate, they are not even food." Chiun lowered his voice. "He told me that when he eats one, his nose runs and his stomach burns. He told me those were the reasons he likes to eat them," Chiun confided.

"I am hungry," Pavel complained. "If we find the warhead soon, could we stop for tacos?"

"I will kill this Russian before I will allow myself to be a witness to his perverted acts,'' Chiun said loudly enough for Pavel to hear.

The sun began to rise, flooding the eastern sky with hot red light. It was a pretty sight, but it made Remo think of a nuclear explosion in slow motion, so he drove faster.

The truck with the warhead was where it was supposed to be. Parked in front of FOES headquarters, it might have been any unmarked delivery van except for the black blots on each side where the nuclear radiation symbols had been painted out.

The two people who had driven the weapon-carrying van jumped out of the truck with relief when Amanda and the others joined them.

''We've got trouble,'' Amanda told them both in a grim voice. ''The World Master says to ditch the FOES van somewhere. Anywhere. It's known.''

The driver nodded and took the van down the street, and came back on foot several minutes later.

''Good,'' Amanda said. ''Now everyone get inside and wait in the office.''

Amanda got back into the car, biting her lip. It was growing light now, and the air had that early morning coolness that Amanda loved as a child but hardly ever experienced anymore.

''They still accept your orders. Good,'' the World Master said.

Amanda did not face him. Instead, she spoke with her face averted, as if to deny his existence at the same time that she held a conversation with him.

''That Remo will be following us,'' Amanda said.

''Yes. He is dangerous. Very dangerous. The old Oriental is not. He believes whatever I tell him. But we must deal with this Remo for our plan to succeed.''

''You—you still intend to detonate the warhead,'' Amanda said flatly.

''It is the only way now. For the American people to be

made to call for the removal of all nuclear weapons, it will take an unforgettable demonstration. This will take time. I cannot activate the warhead without time and tools.''

"Broken Arrow?" Amanda asked, holding back tears.

"Yes, the location I have told you about. It is fortunate that I had prepared this place for an emergency such as this. You know where it will be found from the description I gave you. Order the others to drive the warhead to that location.''

"What—what about me?"

"You will remain here, waiting. This Remo will arrive soon. It will be your job to let him locate you. Once that is done, you will convince him that the warhead is in this city and that you will lead him to it. When he is off his guard, you will kill him. Are these instructions clear to you, Preparation Group Leader Bull?''

The voice, so different from the one Amanda had been used to taking orders from, sounded macabre and cynical asking that question. But Amanda answered as she always had.

"Yes, I understand that part. What about the Oriental?"

"Kill him, too."

"That man who said he was claiming your ship for his government—the one with the accent. What about him?" Amanda asked woodenly.

The World Master paused for so long before he answered that Amanda was about to repeat the question.

"If Pavel Zarnitsa is with them, then he must die, too. For he may have ruined everything."

CHAPTER SIXTEEN

It was all up to her now, Amanda told herself as she stared out the window of FOES headquarters and watched the van carrying the warhead disappear from sight. She felt ill, and the illness was nothing less than a raw fear, but she steeled herself. There were doubts and questions in her mind. There were things that didn't add up anymore, and seemed as if they could never add up. It was possible that the World Master had lied to her about certain things— lied to them all, in fact. There was no escaping that.

But he was still the World Master, Amanda believed. He was still the emissary of a wonderful civilization from far beyond the stars, come to bring peace to this war-torn planet. If he had lied at times, or if his methods seemed harsh, then it was only because his goal was so important. It was justifiable, Amanda told herself. Yes, when it came to saving the Earth from self-destruction, then the end truly justified the means.

Even if that meant obliterating Oklahoma City when the time came.

She had been foolish to doubt the World Master. Why, hadn't he told her that he would be leaving for his Broken Arrow headquarters by himself? Through a method of travel that didn't involve cars or any other vehicles? Yes, that was what he had said. And there on the street below sat the car in which Amanda had left him sitting. See? He didn't need it to get where he was going.

"Teleportation," Amanda said aloud. "I'll bet he's

going by teleportation. Sure! If they can do it on 'Star Trek,' they can do it on—''

Amanda's voice choked off. Below, the huddled figure of the World Master surreptitiously left the back of the car and slipped into the driver's seat.

The car left the curb, dragging a long worm of exhaust in its trail.

"If you don't know where to look," Pavel Zarnitsa was saying, "how are you going to find the nuclear device before it goes off?"

"I know where to look," Remo said, as they drove through the streets of Oklahoma City. "It's somewhere in this town."

"This is not a small place," Pavel pointed out.

"We'll find it," Remo insisted.

"How?" Chiun whispered to him.

"We'll find it," Remo repeated unconvincingly.

"Try the ENEMIES office," Chiun suggested.

"FOES. Not ENEMIES. FOES."

Chiun shrugged. "There is a difference?"

Remo parked in front of the Stigman Building, where the offices of the Flying Object Evaluation Center were. He was tired of visiting the place, and it was probably a waste of time, but he had no other logical place to look for a warhead. As the Russian had rightly said, Oklahoma City was a big place.

"You stay here with him, Chiun," Remo said, indicating the Russian.

"Yes," Chiun agreed. "I will protect this vehicle. With his taste, this one may attempt to eat the seats."

Remo went up the steps to the office. Before he opened the door, his sensitive nostrils detected an odor familiar to him. A human odor that was a distinctive blend of soap and shampoo mingled with perspiration, which itself was distinctive because it was the product of an individual's unique physiological makeup and dietary habits.

The blonde. Amanda Bull.

Remo eased the door open. The room beyond was empty. With a supple grace, he worked his way through the crack in the door and closed it soundlessly. The door leading to the inner office was ajar. Remo made for it. He might have been a wisp of cigarette smoke floating through the room for all the sound he made.

Amanda Bull was waiting for him.

"Oh," she said. "You surprised me." Her voice sounded odd. Remo couldn't tell why at first, then it came to him. She wasn't using her I'm-the-boss-here-and-you-better-know-it voice. She was acting.

"Yeah, I do that a lot," Remo told her, looking for weapons. Her hands were empty, but she stood with her right hand against her hip and slightly back. It was not calm, nor did it exhibit any of the expected nervous habits people showed with their hands. It hovered. There was a weapon at the small of her back.

"Well, I guess you got me," Amanda said.

"Guess so." Remo got to within a few paces of her.

"Uh . . . I suppose you want to know where it is?" Amanda said.

"That's right," Remo said quietly.

"It's here—in Oklahoma City, that is. Hidden where no one can find it."

"Except you?" Remo suggested.

"Yes, except me. I guess I'll have to take you to it."

"Good idea," Remo said. "Why don't you lead the way?"

Amanda began to lead Remo to the door, but Remo caught her elbow and, using his own body as a pivot, swept her half around and pushed her back against the desk. She hit the edge of the desk with the small of her back and said, "Oof," when the impact forced the air from her lungs.

Remo was against her body before she could react, his left arm catching her right, and his right hand found the gun holstered at the small of her back. He felt it, threw the safety to the "on" position but left it there.

"What . . . what are you doing?" Amanda demanded hotly.

Remo didn't answer. His deep eyes gazed into her gray ones, and Amanda felt a shiver course through her body that was less one of fear than it was a sexual reflex. She had never felt anything like the electricity that seemed to jump from Remo's finger to her body. Involuntarily, her breathing increased.

Remo's lips found hers before she could protest—if in fact she intended to protest. His tongue darted out and, closing her eyes, Amanda's mouth yielded, tasted, and replied in kind.

Amanda felt the hard fingers brush her swaying body through the material of her black jumpsuit. The fingers were hard like the blunt noses of bullets, yet they touched and kneaded her with just the right combination of strength and gentleness.

Not thinking of anything but those fingers, Amanda let herself sink back into the desk top, where Remo's fingers worked her wrists until she felt her pulse quicken. Then Remo's manipulations became a long, delicious blur in Amanda Bull's mind until she felt the front zipper of her jumpsuit ease down. And then Remo was inside her, exciting her, pleasing her, questioning her.

"The warhead," Remo asked through the white noise of her pleasure. "Where is it really?"

"Aahhh . . . later," Amanda moaned.

"Now, or I'll stop."

"Uhh—no, don't stop! Please don't stop. Feels . . . good."

"Only good?" Remo asked.

"Meant great—feels great!"

"There's a lot more to come," Remo said, "but only if you answer the question." Remo paused for a fraction of a second, which caused Amanda to grab him violently and begin grinding her body against his frantically.

"No! I'll tell!" Amanda cried. "It's at Broken Arrow. In an oil field."

"Where exactly?" Remo asked, resuming his rhythms.

"Off highway—uhh—Broken Arrow Expressway—"

"The rest of them there?"

"Oohh—oow, yes! Yes, yes! Yessss." But Amanda was no longer answering the question. She was shuddering in the first real climax of her life and was oblivious to everything but the response of her body to that climax.

She was still breathing heavily when she finally opened her eyes and saw Remo Williams standing there with a bored expression on his face, his clothes already replaced.

Amanda zipped up hastily before she got back on her feet.

"It—it was never like that before," she said foolishly.

Remo nodded.

"I told you everything, didn't I?"

Remo nodded again. The disinterest on his dead features was plain. He had used her, Amanda realized. He had given her pleasure such as she had never before experienced—sexual bliss that left her still trembling—but it meant nothing to him.

Amanda screamed. "You bastard!" And she pulled her pistol from the small of her back, aimed once, and pulled the trigger.

Nothing happened.

"Check the safety," Remo said coolly, a spark of humor in the shadows that were his eyes.

The safety was on, Amanda saw. She tried to thumb it off, but it wouldn't budge. She tried again, this time breaking her thumbnail.

"I jammed it," Remo told her. "You'll never get it loose."

"*You bastard*!" Amanda screeched again, and threw the weapon.

Remo weaved on his feet, and the useless pistol looked as if it had gone out of its way to avoid hitting him, rather than vice versa.

Amanda Bull tore out of the office, sobbing. Remo counted the number of photographs of flying saucers on the walls, and didn't leave until he got to 67.

"You let the woman escape?" Chiun asked when Remo rejoined him in the waiting car.

"Yeah," Remo replied. "She told me where the warhead really is, but I figured if I let her go, she'd try to warn the others and lead us to it quicker than if I tried to follow her directions."

Remo coasted down the street slowly.

"She went left," Chiun directed.

Remo steered the car to the left. There was no sign of Amanda Bull, but then a brown van pulled onto the street ahead, and Remo recognized its custom body. It was the official FOES van, which Amanda had retrieved from where it had been ditched earlier.

"We have them, no?" Pavel asked.

"Let's hope," Remo said.

"Where is she going?" Pavel wanted to know.

"Place is called Broken Arrow," Remo told him.

"Broken Arrow? See? I was right: I have helped you, but you wouldn't listen," Zarnitsa said.

"I'm not listening now," Remo said.

CHAPTER SEVENTEEN

When the Homestead Act opened up Oklahoma in the last century, the area called Broken Arrow had boasted of only two natural features: osage and Indians. Then the homesteaders came and started their cattle ranches and farms. Neither the osage nor the Indians vanished. They just sort of blended into the background. Broken Arrow had been a good place to raise beef. There was plenty of wide-open space and it was a short trek to nearby Tulsa, where cattle could be sold or shipped by rail to the hungry East.

By all rights, Broken Arrow should still be that way, and it would be if the cattlemen hadn't found the land bad for farming. It was bad all around. In time, the cattlemen sold off their land and tried again in Arizona or Wyoming. Others, not as young or perhaps more stubborn, stayed on and were still there when the first oil was struck. But not many of them. So few, in fact, that even the Indians got to share in the oil boom. And so what was once cattle-grazing territory vibrated to the *chug* and creak of the oil derrick.

By all rights, Broken Arrow should have remained a booming oil town, but even that did not last, as more of the black stuff was pumped out of the ground to be shipped to the oil-hungry East. While the wells did not always run dry, the ability of men to pump all of the oil out of the ground was not absolute. And so, one by one, some of the oil fields were shut down, not for lack of prod-

162

uct, but because the oil lay so far underground, it could not be tapped.

The building stood in the middle of one of these abandoned fields, among the silent and forgotten spidery towers and pipelines and the overpowering smell of crude. It didn't belong there, but then it looked as if it didn't belong anywhere.

For one thing, it was blue—except for the door, which was a simple white panel on one side. There were no windows or any other ordinary features. In fact, there were no sides in the true sense because the structure was built along the lines of an Eskimo igloo and looked vaguely like a giant seashell lying on its side. But even that didn't describe the thing accurately.

It was unusual enough that Amanda recognized it for what it was immediately even though she had not been given a description of the World Master's emergency retreat, just its general location.

Amanda pulled the van off the road and walked through the scrub oak until she got to the white door. There was no sign of any other vehicle, which struck her as peculiar even in her present state, which was one of high agitation.

The door slid aside as soon as she got near it, and she entered the structure. It was dark inside. The walls felt smooth to her touch, like the bottom of a Teflon-coated frying pan. Amanda followed the wall.

"Stop, Amanda Bull," the baritone voice of the individual Amanda knew only as the World Master said. "You have come far enough. Report your success."

"I—I can't," Amanda said in the gloom. "I tried . . . oh, honestly, I tried. But everything went . . . wrong. Everything has been going wrong all along."

"Cease crying. Continue."

Amanda swallowed. Somehow the darkness made her feel worse than she had been feeling. It seemed to enwrap her.

"I told him the warhead was in the city, but—he

tricked me. He found out the truth. I couldn't kill him—I tried to, but I couldn't—but I got away. I managed to get away somehow.''

"I expected that," the voice intoned.

"You did?"

"Of course. You were no match for this Remo. I expected him to lead or follow you here. This is where I will defeat him, for this place is designed to defeat any intruder.''

"What about the warhead? Where is it?"

"The warhead has been activated and positioned. It will detonate in the city of Tulsa within three hours.''

"Good, I guess," Amanda said sickly. "What about the others? Are they here?''

"Their usefulness has been fulfilled. Preparation Group Two has been rewarded. Just as Preparation Group One was . . .''

"Dead?" Amanda asked weakly. "All of them?"

"All that remains is their brave leader," the World Master said ironically. And he laughed like a ghoul.

Remo waited for Amanda to disappear into the strange blue structure before he left the car, which he had parked in the early morning sunlight at the edge of the abandoned oil field.

"I am coming," Chiun said, stepping out of the car, too.

"No," Remo said. "You've got to stay with the Russian. Smith's orders, remember?''

Chiun shook his head firmly. "Emperor Smith's orders are that I am responsible for him. That does not mean I am to be his babysitter.''

"We can't take him with us," Remo said. He was worried that Chiun might complicate matters when it came to a showdown with the World Master.

"We will lock him in the trunk," Chiun said, dragging Pavel Zarnitsa out of the back seat.

"I protest," Pavel said.

"Me, too," Remo said. "He might escape."

"Then I will incapacitate his legs so he cannot escape," Chiun returned. "It is important that I accompany you, Remo. I have unfinished business."

"That's what I was afraid of," Remo grumbled. He turned to the Russian. "What'll it be? The trunk or your kneecaps?"

"I think I will be very comfortable in the trunk," Pavel said through a forced smile as they put him in the trunk.

There wasn't much cover near the round building. Remo and Chiun moved along the oil rigs until they were as close as they could get without being exposed. Remo, seeing no activity, began to move forward.

"Wait," said Chiun. "It is a maze. I recognize the form."

"So?" said Remo. "There's the door, and I don't see any guards. Let's rush it."

"Yes," Chiun snapped. "Let us rush the door. Let us blunder to our deaths now, while there is still daylight. Why should we wait and carefully plan our attack when we can go impatiently to our deaths and end this terrible suspense?"

"All right, all right," Remo said. "I'm listening."

Chiun sat down amid the wild grass and placidly waited until Remo, heaving a sigh of exasperation, sat beside him. Chiun gestured toward the blue building.

"Behold this structure, Remo," he said. "What does it say to you?"

"Say? It doesn't say anything."

"Wrong. Nothing in the universe is silent. All things have voices." Chiun pulled a long blade of grass from the earth and held it up so that Remo could see its roots. "This lowly blade of grass speaks to me. By the lack of dirt in its roots and by its yellow color, it tells me that if I had not plucked it and put it out of its misery, it would have withered away painfully."

"So?" Remo looked around him. The thought had occurred to him that this might be a grazing area and he hoped he hadn't stepped or sat in anything unpleasant.

"So this, dull one. That structure, by its very form, tells me that it is a maze designed to create difficulties for any who enter it. For it is a snail maze. There is only one entrance, one exit and one path, which winds around itself and ends in a central chamber."

"That doesn't sound like a maze to me," Remo said doubtfully. "A maze has a lot of passages and blind turns and things like that."

"That is a Western maze. A confused pattern designed by confused minds to confuse minds even more confused than they."

"Huh?" said Remo, who was suddenly confused himself.

"See?" smiled the Master of Sinanju, having proven his point by example. "A snail maze is an Eastern maze. Even the Russian would have recognized it. Now this is a pure maze. It is designed to force an intruder along a certain path, which is a spiral. The spiral path slows down the intruder so that he falls victim to traps or interception. Because there is no direct path, the intruder cannot by accident find a short cut. To one who is allowed safe passage or who knows the key, entrance is a simple matter. To intruders, it is often fatal.

"I think I get it," Remo said. "This maze is designed to protect the man in its center."

"Yes. It is he who controls the traps set along the path."

"The World Master," Remo said. "He's probably got the warhead in that central chamber, too. Little Father, you know it is important to recover that warhead."

Chiun nodded.

"It may be that we will have to fight this World Master . . ." Remo said hesitantly.

Chiun looked momentarily uncomfortable. "Once," he

said, "there was a Master named Huk, who was summoned to the court of a king of Assyria."

"Come on, Chiun," Remo interrupted. "We're wide open here. Do we have to go into a legend now?"

"No, insolent one. We can squander the lesson of Huk, if your American genius has enabled you to understand what lies within the snail maze."

Remo folded his arms and was silent.

"Now, this king of Assyria was greatly worried. For he had heard rumors that a neighboring king was preparing to make war against him. A great warrior was the Assyrian king, and he possessed a mighty army which feared no enemy. But the reputation of this enemy king was great, for none had ever seen him, and it was rumored that he was not like other men. This king lived in a fortress composed of seven concentric rings surrounding his throne room. Each ring had its own guards, and each ring had a single advisor who controlled his ring. When someone wished to bring a message to this king, it was first given to the advisor who controlled the outermost ring, who passed the message to the next ring, until it had gone through all seven rings. Only the advisor of the innermost ring was allowed to deal directly with this king. For beheading was the penalty for any who set eyes upon him. Only he knew what his king looked like, and it was from him that the rumors about the king came. And these tales likewise passed through the ring until when they reached the ears of the king's subjects, they made the king seem to be more like a god than a man.

"Great legends grew up around this king whom no one saw. That he was eight feet tall with skin the color and hardness of bronze. Some said he possessed three eyes, and the third eye could burn the life from any living thing. Others told that this king had four arms, each of which could wield any weapon with skill. It was also said that this king sometimes walked among his subjects unseen, for he knew the secret of invisibility, and all manner of

strange happenings in his kingdom were explained in that
way.

"Now, these stories were told to Huk, whom the
Assyrian king had contracted to penetrate the enemy
king's fortress and dispose of him there, thus ending the
threat of war. The Master Huk then journeyed to this fortress, which was in the land of the Medes, and on that
journey, he thought long on the legends surrounding this
king. Thus, by the time he stood before that fortress, he
was frightened, for in truth he knew not what to expect
beyond those walls. Not knowing which of the many powers this king actually possessed, he had to prepare to fight
someone who possessed all of those powers. And not even
the Master of Sinanju might prevail against such a one as
described.

"But the Master entered the fortress and dispatched
the advisor and guards of the first ring. Then he passed
into the second ring, whose guards were better trained.
And these he vanquished, too. The third ring was more difficult still, but Huk prevailed.

"Ring after ring the Master Huk passed through, each
one more difficult than the last, until he at last came to
the seventh ring, tired and wary. When he had vanquished
the guards of the seventh ring, he captured its advisor, the
one who alone was privileged to meet directly with the
king. And outside the very throne room itself, Huk
demanded of this advisor, 'What manner of being lies
beyond this door?'

"And this man replied in this way, 'Beyond this door
lies a man unlike any other.' And that was all the advisor
would say, so Huk dispatched him and prepared to enter
the throne room. And he trembled, for the unknown lay
waiting for him, and while the Master of Sinanju fears
nothing that he knows, only a fool does not fear what is
not known. Remember this, Remo, for it is important.

"Putting aside his fear, Huk entered the throne room,
where he found the king seated upon his throne. At first,

he could not believe his sight and demanded, 'Are you the king I have come to slay?'

"And the king—for it was he—said to him, 'I am king of this land. But please do not harm me, for I am no match for you.'

"This caused the Master of Sinanju to laugh, for the king's words were true. The king was a mere dwarf whose limbs were twisted by deformity. And Huk knew then that his fears were groundless and caused by legends deliberately created by the king and his advisors, who had concealed the truth through cunning methods so that this king would be obeyed by his awestruck subjects, who would otherwise have deposed him. And so, laughing at his own fears, Huk dragged this drawf king out of his fortress and exposed him for all to see.''

"Then he let him go?'' Remo asked.

"No. Then he slew him in front of his subjects as a warning to any who would dare attack Assyria.''

"Oh,'' said Remo, who knew there was a point to their story but couldn't see it. "That fortress was a snail maze, right?''

"Wrong.''

"But the way Huk got to the throne room applies to the snail maze?''

"Oh, Remo, you are hopeless. That has nothing to do with it.''

Remo looked perplexed. Finally, he said, "I give up. What's the point?''

Chiun stood up abruptly. "Never mind,'' he said peevishly. "I have wasted a good legend. So be it. You will learn the lesson of Huk the hard way.''

Remo got to his feet. Why couldn't Chiun just come out and make his points in plain English? Sometimes these legends could be a royal pain.

"Okay, how are we going to take this snail maze?'' Remo asked.

Chiun looked toward the maze, measured a distance

from the single white door to a point directly north of it
with his eyes, and walked toward that point. Remo followed.

"The snail maze can be breached," Chiun was saying,
"and because of that possibility, there is always an escape
tunnel which leads from the center to the outside. It is
always a prescribed distance north . . . ah, here." He
upended a flat boulder, disclosing a dark hole. "This tunnel will be a straight line longer than the spiral path, but
it will be guarded at its other end, Remo."

"Yeah?"

"One of us must take the snail maze to keep this Hopak
Kay busy. The other will go by the tunnel."

"Wanna flip for it?" Remo suggested.

"No," Chiun said. "I do not. I will let you take the
snail maze because you can learn from it. Remember that
there are traps along the way. The rest you must discover
for yourself."

"Okay, Little Father," Remo said, moving off. "Last
one in has to cook tonight."

Pavel Zarnitsa had read in *Izvestia* that American cars
were badly made in comparison to the Russian Volga.
After ten minutes of trying to spring the trunk lid lock, he
was beginning to wonder. It seemed awfully sturdy. The
hinges were strong, too, so he gave up on those, as well.

It might have been better to stay put, but the American and the Korean were obviously agents for the United
States government, who would not treat a compromised
KGB agent with the same politeness given to Russian dig-
nitaries found stealing military secrets. It would be
prison, not expulsion, for Pavel Zarnitsa.

So Pavel tried another tack. He tore at the carpeting
that separated the trunk space from the back of the rear
seat. It came loose. Behind it was a partition, which also
came loose and exposed the back seat itself. When this
was forced, there was a clear opening into the back seat.

Pavel crawled out of the trunk and stepped from the car. He was free, but he had no intention of running. There was still the matter of the strange creature from another world who had called him by name. Pavel Zarnitsa intended to solve that mystery.

The white door opened automatically for Remo when he approached it. He could sense the remote cameras watching his every move. He stepped into the blue building, and the door closed after him.

Remo found himself in a curving corridor, white and smooth and winding to his left. He began to walk. Light came from indirect ceiling panels. There seemed to be no danger. In fact, the curving corridor reminded him a little of walking through a fun house back in Palisades Amusement Park, where his orphanage had once been taken on an outing. He had only gone a few feet when he noticed that the natural curve of the path prevented him from seeing more than a few feet ahead or behind him. More disturbingly, he realized that the path was forcing him to move along a continuous outside line. In Sinanju, there were two forms of attack—the outside attack, which was a circle, and the inside attack, which was a line. Remo realized then that any attack would come from ahead or behind, and from the right outer wall, where an inside attack would be the only defense.

The first attack came from the right. Three knives rammed out of the wall at knee level to cripple his legs. But Remo caught the preliminary sound of a concealing panel flopping back and reversed himself in time. The knives embedded themselves in the opposite wall.

Remo walked on.

The second attack came when Remo began to feel himself favor his left, even though he knew that side was probably safe. He tried to avoid hugging the wall, but the spiral path wouldn't let him. It had started to tilt slightly to the left so Remo had to walk that way, as if one of his legs was shorter than the other.

Then a ball of flame appeared at his back, forcing Remo forward. He ran, aware that the flame might be more of a prod than a direct threat. And because of that awareness, he did not crash headlong into the almost invisible pane of glass, which, had he struck it, would have shattered into dangerous razorlike shards.

Remo found the edges of the pane and scored it using one very short but hard fingernail. A kick sent the pane to the ground, where it broke harmlessly on the floor. Chiun would have liked that.

Remo continued on with more confidence—or perhaps because the spiral shrank as it got closer to the center, he found himself moving faster. He tried to slow down, but when everything in two directions seemed to curve into infinity, judging distance and speed became difficult.

Remo heard the next obstacle before he saw it. Someone moaned just ahead. Putting his back to the left wall, he inched sideways toward the sound so he'd be less of a target.

Amanda Bull lay on her back in a pool of blood. Remo knelt beside her, and she opened her eyes.

Amanda coughed a bubble of blood. "Tricked . . ." she gasped. "He tricked me. Tricked all of us."

"Where are the others?" Remo asked.

"Dead . . . all . . . dead . . ."

"The warhead—do you know where I can find it?"

"Tulsa," Amanda said with effort. "In truck. Will go off . . . three hours. Look—look for plain truck with blotches of paint on sides. Find—"

"Easy," Remo told her.

"He—shot—me," Amanda continued, her gray eyes fixed on the ceiling. "I . . . trusted him and he *shot* me . . . I was such a jerk. Believing a man."

Then she died.

"That's the biz, sweetheart," Remo said and moved on. "They should have drowned you at birth."

The Master of Sinanju was almost there. The tunnel was damp and cool, and he could feel it in his bones despite his robes. Ahead, chinks of light indicated a door not properly fitted. That light had been the only illumination in the blackness of the tunnel.

Chiun paused to listen. He heard nothing ahead of him, but after a space, he heard slow footsteps *behind* him. Not Remo. The Russian. He had escaped and followed the Master of Sinanju.

Chiun, all but invisible in the darkness, pushed himself against the earthen side of the tunnel and allowed the Russian to pass by him. Let the Russian blunder through the door on his own, if that was his wish. If he was not killed immediately, then Chiun would know that it was safe to proceed.

Seeing the old Korean disappear into the ground several hundred yards from the odd-shaped building, Pavel Zarnitsa naturally assumed that Chiun and Remo had both gone into the tunnel. He waited briefly, then entered the tunnel. The Americans would blaze the trail for him so he could safely follow.

The tunnel was black as a Politburo limousine, and Pavel was forced to feel his way along the walls, which seemed to go on forever until the vague outline of a door showed ahead. There was no sign of the two Americans. Good. They had already gone in. Now Pavel Zarnitsa would go in, too.

He put his shoulder to the yielding door.

The room was circular. Fluorescent lights flickered bluely from the ceiling, which gave the room something of the aspect of a hospital operating room. Or a morgue.

There was a small control console opposite the place where Pavel found himself. A figure was seated at that console, watching a television screen on which Remo Williams could be seen moving down a winding corridor. The figure was dressed in a long purple garment something like a monk's cassock but without the cowl. Above its collar rose the figure's head, which was a pinkish bulb twice the size of a human's and the color of the inside of someone's eyelid. Pavel could not see the World Master's face, who sat with his back to the Russian, but he did see the twin sets of spindly arms hanging uselessly from the armholes of the purple garment.

Two other arms—human ones—projected from the front of the garment to manipulate the console buttons.

Pavel eased forward, trying to make no sound. But he made a sound.

The World Master turned in his chair, causing his false arms to rattle like kindling. But Pavel wasn't thinking of them, or of the unearthly face that now faced his own. He was thinking of the familiar baritone voice that came from the slit mouth beneath the single fisheye set in the center of the World Master's pink face.

"Pavel! You fool. You stupid fool—you do not belong here!"

"Chuzhoi!" Pavel croaked incredulously. "What is this? What—"

"Idiot," the expressionless face said. "You have stumbled upon a GRU operation. The greatest of all time."

"No," Pavel said hollowly. "You cannot do this. Exploding a nuclear weapon in the United States is wrong. You—"

"You will not stop me," the other said, drawing a revolver. "I cannot allow you to interfere."

Pavel stepped back in shock. "You would shoot me? *I am your brother!*"

The ceiling changed. It was no longer smooth, Remo saw. Instead, for about six feet, it was perforated with hundreds of tiny holes. Beyond that, just visible around the bend, the ceiling was smooth again.

Remo became a blur, and thus sped through the danger zone before any of the acid that squirted from above could hit him. He looked back and saw the acid spatter and blacken the floor. Fumes curled up and reached toward him. Before Remo could move on, he saw another perforated section of ceiling revealed just ahead. It, too, began raining acid. And the acid formed puddles, which spilled in the direction of Remo's feet.

There was barely time for the fact that he was trapped to sink in when Remo heard the sound of gunshots through the walls followed by a trailing scream.

"*Aiiieeeee!*"

Chiun. That scream was Chiun's.

Remo ran forward three steps, putting him on an outside line, and let it carry him through the sheet metal wall. The wall screeched like the amplified sound of a nail pulled from wood as Remo's hands pierced it and bent it outward.

He was in the next corridor, really a continuation of the single spiral. Remo got back on the outside line, and tore through the next wall. He stumbled right into a trap. A hand grenade dropped from a ceiling trap by a string, which pulled the pin out.

Remo grabbed the grenade and threw it down the corridor and threw himself in the opposite direction. The explosion hurt his eardrums even though he'd remembered to open his mouth wide to equalize the pressure that might otherwise have damaged them.

Picking himself up, Remo went through the last wall as if it were a sheet of foil and found himself in the central chamber.

The first thing he saw was Chiun, looking horrified, standing with his back against one wall and looking down at two bodies lying on the floor. Chiun saw Remo.

"I think it is dead," Chiun squeaked. "I may have killed it, but I am not certain. Oh, Remo, isn't it horrible?"

Remo looked at the still form of the World Master, whose encephalitic head lay at too sharp an angle to his body for his neck not to be broken. A single fisheye stared up sightlessly, and the many arms, both human and not, which splayed from the creature's body made it look like some deformed spider.

Remo knelt beside the body, while Chiun all but jumped onto the console chair like a caricature of a woman who has seen a mouse.

"Is it dead, Remo?" Chiun asked.

Remo touched the pinkish head and felt the slickness of plastic. He pulled the head loose to reveal a human head whose strong features and black hair resembled those of Pavel Zarnitsa's—even in death.

"Relax, Chiun. It's only a disguise."

"Are you certain?" Chiun asked doubtfully. "But when he saw the truth, he shook himself and stepped forward confidently. "Why, of course it is a disguise, Remo. How could it not be?"

Remo ignored that and asked, "What happened here?"

"This Russian freed himself and followed me, but I tricked him," Chiun said, pointing to Pavel Zarnitsa, who was either dead or very close to it. "I let him pass before me. He surprised this—this insect—and they quarrelled. The insect shot him, and I felled the insect with a single blow to its neck. Then I saw its face. . . ."

Remo went to Pavel Zarnitsa. The Russian was bleeding to death. He would not live long, but for the moment he did live.

Pavel opened his eyes. "He . . . is dead?"

Remo nodded.

"Is . . . my brother," Pavel said. "Chuzhoi . . . Zarnitsa. Younger brother . . . with GRU. You know GRU? He—he should have been KGB. Now . . . is dead. I am . . . dead, too. No? He called me fool. He is . . . fool.

He would kill . . . own brother for stupid GRU plan . . . Listen. You must—must find warhead before—''

"I know where it is," Remo told him, coming to his feet. "I'm going to have to leave you."

Pavel closed his eyes. "I will be dead when you return."

"I know," Remo said. And he and Chiun left through the underground tunnel.

"The warhead's in Tulsa, Chiun," Remo said as they piled into the car. "We've got maybe two hours before it goes."

"You learned the snail maze?"

Remo nodded. "The trick is not to follow the path."

"Good. You have learned something for a change."

Finding the truck was the easy part. It stood on a side street in downtown Tulsa near the university. Remo recognized it from Amanda Bull's description. A plain truck except for the paint splotches, which hid the black and yellow nuclear emblems on its sides.

Remo broke the latch and threw open the cargo door. The warhead was inside. It looked small and unimpressive for the damage it could wreak.

"There it is," Remo said. "I'd better call Smith."

"There is no time," Chiun said levelly. "I must act quickly."

"You? Chiun, this calls for an expert. If you make a mistake, you'll blow us up."

Chiun ignored him. "There is no time to acquire the correct oil, so I must find another way," he said to himself as he felt the cone projection, which was the most distinguishing feature of the warhead.

"Maybe we should drive it out of the city, where it'll do less damage when it blows," Remo suggested.

"It will not explode," Chiun said.

"Since when do you know anything about nuclear weapons?"

Chiun stopped what he was doing and looked at Remo. "Do you remember the puzzle, Remo?"

"The Rubik's Cube? Sure. But what does that have to do—"

"You could not understand how I was able to solve the cube, even with my eyes closed. But I did. This was possible because everything man makes is given a basic form, a unity of self. When this puzzle was built, its unity of form had all of the little colored squares properly arranged. When the squares are disarranged, the internal unity is disturbed. This has nothing to do with the colored squares, Remo, but with the way the puzzle parts fitted together when it was in unity with itself. To solve this cube, I did not even look at the colored squares, I simply manipulated its parts until I felt those parts achieve unity. The colors took care of themselves."

"You did it by feel, then?"

"Yes. And one day you, too, will be able to accomplish the same thing. It is the same with this device. At the point of its creation, it was not armed. It is armed now and is therefore in disunity. I will undo that disunity now."

"Okay, Little Father. It's your show. I just hope you're right."

Chiun went back to the warhead. It was a complicated mechanism—certainly more complicated than a Rubik's Cube, even if the combinations were fewer. The consequences of even a single error were all the greater, however . . .

Remo stood guard outside the truck. It was late morning now, and young college students passed by the truck frequently. They had no idea that they were only a few feet away from a nuclear weapon that could end their studies and their lives in a single white-hot flash of fire. It was an eerie sensation for Remo Williams. He wanted to warn them away, but he knew that no matter how far they ran or drove, they would not escape the nuclear blast. So what was the use? Let them enjoy themselves—while they could.

Almost an hour dragged past, and Remo stuck his head inside the truck. "How's it coming?" he asked anxiously.

But the Master of Sinanju, intent upon his work, did not answer him.

Remo returned to his thoughts. What would Smith do if they all went up? Would he—

"*Run, Remo!*" Chiun shouted suddenly, and came out of the truck like a shot.

"Huh?" Remo said, startled.

"*Run!*"

Remo took off, Chiun at his side. Together, they rounded a corner just as a great explosion echoed behind them. Remo prepared for the flash that would obliterate them both . . .

"It is all right now," Chiun said, coming to a stop.

"It exploded. The warhead exploded. Why aren't we dead?"

"We are not dead thanks to the skill of the Master of Sinanju," Chiun said as he led Remo back to the smoking ruin that was the truck.

Remo looked at the truck. "I don't get it. Was it a dud?"

"No," Chiun told him. "It was almost our deaths. The fools who built that device built it so that once armed, its unity could not be reestablished."

"Probably something to do with the failsafe," Remo suggested.

"Whatever. When I discovered this, Remo, I examined the mechanism to see what made it work. Thus I discovered that in order for the atomic part to work, it must be made to work by an ordinary explosion."

"That's right," Remo said, ignoring the people who had rushed to the scene. "They trigger the nuclear explosion with a regular one. I read that somewhere once."

"I saw that I could not stop the smaller explosive device without possibly causing the bigger explosion. So I ignored that and rendered the atomic part useless. This caused the small explosion."

"For a minute I thought you'd blown it," Remo said. "Not a bad job."

"An excellent job," Chiun corrected. "Next time I will be able to do it with my eyes closed."

"Remind me to be out sick that day," Remo said.

CHAPTER EIGHTEEN

Later that night, they met with Dr. Harold W. Smith at the farm owned by the late Ethel Sump.

"Whaddya say, Smitty?" Remo said when Smith arrived.

"Remo. Master of Sinanju," Smith said curtly.

"Hail, Emperor Smith. What news?"

"I've managed to tie up most of the loose ends of this matter. The remains of the warhead have been disposed of, and a story planted in the Tulsa papers to cover the explosion. You did an excellent job dealing with the warhead, Master of Sinanju. The president is grateful."

Chiun bowed. "Perhaps his gratitude will manifest itself in interesting ways," he suggested.

"Eh?"

"What Chiun is trying to say, Smitty," Remo put in, "is that he figures he deserves a bonus for saving Tulsa."

"A modest bonus," Chiun added. "I have learned that there are 432,800 people who live in that place. Perhaps one gold coin per life saved would be appropriate . . ."

"We will discuss this later," Smith said, frowning. "I'd like to examine this so-called flying saucer first."

"Not much left, is there?" Remo said as they stood over the cool slag.

Smith probed the metallic remains with a penknife. "I ran a check on Chuzhoi Zarnitsa before I left Folcroft. He belonged to the GRU, a Russian intelligence rival of the KGB. We hadn't known he was in this country. As best as

I've been able to determine, this Chuzhoi was not acting on direct orders of the Soviet Union. It isn't always possible to know anything for certain in this area, but this plot to destroy our missile defense system was apparently his own. It may have been sanctioned by the GRU, but that's as high as the orders emanated. Zarnitsa had no support personnel in this country—except for his American dupes.''

"What about the blonde?" Remo asked.

"Her name was really Amanda Bull. She was the first to be recruited. Her background is not extraordinary. In fact, none of the FOES members were anything but ordinary people.''

"They were amateurs, Emperor," Chiun offered. "I dealt with them while Remo was ill. They could do nothing correctly. Especially the woman.''

"Really? Then you were with them when they attacked the missile base. Perhaps you could explain how these amateurs were able to breach our security and destroy that missile.''

"Because they were vicious killers who would stop at nothing,'' Chiun said instantly.

"But you just said they were incompetent," Smith said.

Chiun shrugged. "What do you expect? They are Americans, and therefore inconsistent.''

Smith regarded Chiun with momentary perplexity. "In any case," he resumed, "none of them survived, which is probably for the best. We've recovered the bodies of all concerned and have made arrangements so that it appears they all died accidental deaths. The Zarnitsa brothers will be cremated, and as far as the Russians will ever know, they simply disappeared.''

"What about explaining the missile accident?" Remo asked.

"That will be taken care of, too. The disarmament groups will be a problem for a while, but the public has a short memory for such incidents. Gradually, the matter will be forgotten—as long as the full story never gets out.''

''I'm not so sure that's the right thing to do,'' Remo told Smith. ''After all, those crazies did wreck a missile and then steal the warhead. Maybe the public should know how vulnerable this whole nuclear business is. And how nuts those people are.''

Smith didn't bother to look up from his examination of the destroyed flying saucer. ''Fortunately, that's not up to you, Remo. Don't worry, new safeguards will be installed because of what happened out here.''

Remo wasn't sure he agreed, but he let it pass. ''Well, that explains everything except the UFO. What was it?''

Smith got to his feet and brushed hay off his knees. ''This will have to be analyzed first, but I'm reasonably certain that when it is, we will discover that Zarnitsa was operating from a small airship, a dirigible probably. It could float soundlessly, hover, and carry a small complement of people and equipment to do what your flying saucer actually did. The many bright lights probably helped disguise its flimsy construction and the air fans—or whatever they were—which propelled it horizontally for short distances.''

''That would explain why it registered strangely when I got close to it,'' Remo said. ''I was expecting to sense heavy machinery inside, but instead I felt a hollowness. That was because it was filled mostly with gas. But what about those weapons?''

''You already know about the ultrasonic field. The death ray you described to me is probably a laser with a blue filter to give the beam a different look. Most people expect lasers to be red, you know. The whole ship probably ran off storage batteries.''

''It's over, at any rate,'' Remo said. ''The whole crazy thing.''

''And it was crazy,'' Smith agreed. ''They could never

have succeeded in their goal without starting an international crisis. But this whole business of pretending to be an alien from another planet did convince enough people to become a serious matter.''

''Pah! How could anyone believe such a thing?'' Chiun spat.

''I'm glad you weren't fooled, Chiun,'' Remo said dryly. ''It would have been a real disaster if one of us hadn't kept his head.''

Smith looked at them both steadily. ''I have some more details to attend to. You'll hear from me.'' And he left.

''You were trying to tell me that the World Master was a fraud when you recited that legend of Huk and the dwarf king, weren't you?'' Remo asked Chiun after Smith had departed.

''Of course,'' Chiun said. ''I wanted to break the news to you gently, but naturally you missed the point.''

''You knew he was a fake then, but when you crashed in on him, you were pretty freaked out by what you saw.''

Chiun started to walk off. Remo followed. ''I expected to come upon a dwarf, not a man dressed like a cockroach,'' Chiun said innocuously.

''When did you first suspect the truth?''

''I knew it all along.''

''Bull. If you knew it all along you wouldn't have helped that dippy blonde wreck that missile. And if Smith ever figures out it was you who was really responsible for that, he'll probably take the cost out of the next shipment of gold he sends to your village.''

''Do not ever let him know the truth, Remo,'' Chiun admonished. ''I will avoid the subject in the future. Perhaps I will tell Smith that he need not pay a bonus for the saving of that city. Yes, I will tell him that I make a present of Tulsa to him. Perhaps they might erect a statue in my honor instead. One with a plaque which reads, CHIUN, SAVIOR OF TULSA. Yes, I would like that.''

"You still haven't answered my question. When did you really figure out that the World Master was a phoney?"

"If you must know, Remo, I became suspicious upon our second meeting," Chiun said. "This World Master agreed with everything I said. He was very glib. But he was ignorant of the sun source. This made me suspicious, as did the name he gave. No Master would give himself a name like Large Hairy Dog."

"I still don't understand that part. Why did he take a Korean name?"

"He did not. He made up a name. To my ears, which expected that name to be Korean, it sounded like Hopak Kay, which means Large Hairy Dog. I told you his accent was atrocious."

"Yeah, but what tipped you off finally?"

Chiun turned to face Remo Williams. "It was when I asked him about his world. You know he claimed to be from an advanced civilization. When I asked him about the position of assassins in this so-called advanced civilization, he told me there were none, and I knew then he was a despicable liar."

"Because there weren't supposed to be assassins on his planet, you knew he was lying?" Remo demanded.

"Certainly," Chiun beamed. "Who ever heard of an advanced civilization without assassins?"

"Got me," Remo said.

Chiun reached into his ballooning sleeves and brought out his Rubik's Cube.

"And now on to serious things," he said.

Watch for
DATE WITH DEATH
fifty-seventh novel in the exciting
DESTROYER series from
Pinnacle
coming in October!